MATED TO THE WARRIORS

GRACE GOODWIN

Published by Stormy Night Publications and Design, LLC.
www.StormyNightPublications.com

Cover design by Korey Mae Johnson
www.koreymaejohnson.com

Images by The Killion Group and Bigstock/mikiel

1st Print Edition. April 2016

ISBN-13: 978-1530826414

ISBN-10: 1530826411

FOR AUDIENCES 18+ ONLY

This book is intended for adults only. Spanking and other sexual activities represented in this book are fantasies only, intended for adults.

CHAPTER ONE

Hannah Johnson, Interstellar Bride Processing Center, Earth

I was blindfolded, but I could hear the soft hum of several deep male voices whispering around me. I was surrounded. I turned my head left, then right, but I could see nothing, only blackness. Something silky smooth, but liquid like melted chocolate, enclosed my neck like a collar of liquefied heat. Once the circle was complete, my senses were enhanced. The scent of my mate's cock teased the air and I knew he stood before me. I could smell the spicy scent of his arousal. I knew well the exotic taste of his pleasure on my lips. How did I know his taste? How did I know the collar about my neck linked me to him somehow?

I tugged at my bonds, trying to reach him, to taste him, but the thick straps that held my wrists together above my head prevented me from doing so. The desire for my mates and the power of their link to me were strong, but all I could do was stand, naked, and wait.

The scent of my own skin and something strangely metallic flavored the air. I could feel the soft flow of slightly cool air moving over my naked flesh. My legs were in a wide stance. Pulling on the restraints above my head, I tried to step forward, but realized that thick straps around my ankles

1

restrained my movement. I kicked at them, but found that although I had a few inches of leeway, beyond that, I could not budge.

All I could do was wait. My ears strained to hear footsteps, a rustle of clothing, anything to alert me to what was going to happen next. I was confused and uneasy, but my body was eager and aching for my mate's touch.

The thought sent me into a near panic, and my heart pounded so hard I was afraid it was going to explode out of my ribcage.

What was this? Why was I naked? Where the hell was I? This was not what I'd signed up for when I volunteered for the Interstellar Bride Program. I was supposed to be matched to a mate who would be perfect for me, and me alone. I was supposed to be cherished and loved, and…

As if I'd summoned him, a large hand settled on my shoulder and slid up to the side of my neck. Even blindfolded, I could feel the brute strength in that touch, and the sheer size of his palm made me tremble, but not with fear. I knew his touch, somehow, and craved more.

His voice filled my ear from behind, and he pressed the heat of his naked chest to my bare back.

"Do you accept my claim, mate? Do you give yourself to me and my second freely, or do you wish to choose another primary mate?" A deep, baritone voice growled the questions and my pussy grew wet in response to his voice. My mind didn't recognize him, but my body did.

"I accept your claim, warriors." The words flew past my lips, as if I had no control. And, in fact, I did not. I tried to ask a question, to find out where I was, what was going on, but it was like I was in a virtual reality sim. I could feel the heat of the giant male at my back. I could smell my mate's pre-cum teasing me with future pleasures. I could feel the unforgiving metal of the floor beneath my bare feet and the heated glide of liquid silk as it wrapped around my neck. I could hunger and ache and want, but I could not move.

Whatever was going to happen next was completely out

of my control.

"Then we claim you in the rite of naming. You are mine and I shall kill any other warrior who dares to touch you." His hand squeezed softly, wrapping around my neck in the front, a soft but gentle reminder that he was the dominant one, that he could take me, fuck me, make me come—and there was nothing I could do about it.

I didn't want to escape that strength. I wanted more.

I'd chosen this, the Interstellar Bride Program and their selection testing. I vowed I would give my destined mate my trust and my life, utterly and without reservation.

He pressed his lips to the side of my face as the voices I'd heard chanting earlier answered him in a ritual sounding chorus of male voices. "May the gods witness and protect you."

My mate growled behind me and squeezed my throat the slightest bit with his right hand, and my pussy fluttered in welcome. A second pair of large male hands came to rest on the outsides of my thighs, and I knew then that another male knelt before me.

The hungry primary mate at my back held me tightly against his chest as my second man's rough tongue traced its way from the inside of my knee, up my inner thigh, to lick the wet core of me.

My hips jerked forward as his mouth clamped down on my clit. Two very large fingers slid into my pussy as he worked me into a frenzy with his mouth and tongue. I panted for breath and the growling behind me made my knees weak.

"You like his mouth on you?"

I knew, somehow, that he expected an answer, and that there would be no lying. "Yes."

"Come for us, then we will fuck you." His large cock nestled against my bare bottom and I was torn between the desire to press forward onto the sucking tongue that made me squirm, or push back hard to tease the cock pressed to my ass.

I tried to do both, but couldn't move. My captor kept one hand on my neck and another teasing one nipple, then the other, into tight peaks. He tugged them to the edge of pain as the man between my legs fucked me with his fingers and licked my clit so fast, he was better than any vibrator I'd ever used back home.

I moaned. I needed to be filled. Fucked. Claimed. Forever.

I exploded and pressed the back of my head into the giant chest behind me. He belonged to me now, my safe harbor, my mate. When my legs collapsed, he held me up, as I knew he would. He was mine, and I was his.

His voice was practically a purr in my ear. "Very good, we will fuck you now, mate. You belong to us."

Us. Yes. I wanted both of them. "Yes."

The man kneeling on the floor was mine, too. They were both mine.

My ankles were released and I was spun in a circle to face the male behind me. He lifted me off the floor and stepped back. I couldn't see as they freed my wrists. I lowered my arms, settled my wrists at my waist, grateful for the relief in my shoulders as my mate pulled me onto his lap facing him. I felt the huge head of his cock brush my core, and that was the only warning I received before he lifted me, then invaded me with one brutal stroke.

I cried out at the thick feel of him impaling me. He was huge!

I was stuffed so full my pussy ached and so aroused I couldn't think, I could only want. But before long, the familiar pleasurable heat of his pre-cum spread from my pussy to the rest of me and I squirmed, so hot and out of control that if he didn't move soon I was going to beg.

"Now, you shall be claimed. Forever."

His voice vibrated through my body and somehow, I knew what was coming as he leaned backward. He lay flat, pulling me down on top of him with my ass in the air.

Two hands landed on my bare bottom and held me with

a firm, hungry grip. As I leaned forward over my mate, a second man squeezed heated oil into my virgin hole, and I whimpered.

This was what I'd been waiting for, what I'd wanted. What they'd been training me for.

My primary mate shifted below me, rubbing my clit over his hard body and I shuddered, so close to the edge that I felt like a wild animal, my entire focus on the joining of our bodies, and the thick glide of the second cock over my ass.

From behind me, a second voice, deep, solid, and reverent spoke to me. "Do you accept me, mate?"

"Yes!" I tried to lift my ass, to encourage him to move faster. His pre-cum traced a line of wetness on my bare ass cheek, then I felt the arousing fluid practically melt into my skin, driving me higher.

I lay flat on my mate's chest, my hands lifted to his face and waited for my other mate to breach me, to fill me, to make me truly complete.

My mate grabbed my knees and shifted under my legs, spreading my knees farther and bringing my ass up in perfect position for fucking. My knees were still bent, and as he supported my weight, I was bent over and ready for the second cock to fill me up.

"Hurry. Do it now."

Was that my husky voice? I didn't recognize the breathless sound, so filled with desperate hunger.

"I am pleased by your eagerness, but do not attempt to issue orders." A hand landed on my bare ass with a loud smack and I jerked in place as stinging heat spread straight from my ass to my clit. I wiggled my ass, wanting the man behind me to strike again. And again.

I licked my lips as my body clenched down on the cock filling my pussy. "Take me."

Smack.

"Fuck me," I begged.

Smack.

"*Please!*" I moaned as I thrust my hips back for the next

strike of his palm. The mixture of pain and sizzling pleasure was incredible.

Smack.

"Please? Is that all you have to say to us?" My first mate asked the question with his cock buried balls deep inside me.

Oh, I knew what he wanted, and I was tempted to push him further, to feel the hot sting of their domination on my ass again and again. The flash of pain sparked my nerve endings and made my whole body tremble with lust. But I had pushed as far as I dared, and I was so aroused that my pussy actually throbbed, the need to come driving me to the brink of pain. I needed him—them—pounding into me. I needed to be completely filled. "Please, sir."

He didn't answer me with words, but some sign must have passed between them, for the thick head of my second mate's cock pressed against my tight little rosebud, penetrating the outer walls of my virgin ass with remarkable ease. I knew now that the training I'd been put through had been well worth it. The sound that left my throat was one I didn't recognize. After several careful yet masterful strokes, the man behind me stilled, his cock fully embedded in my ass.

I shattered into a million pieces at the connection, came apart and gave them everything. I didn't keep anything for myself.

I surrendered, completely. Wholly. My body belonged to them, my pleasure, my every breath.

As my body clenched and spasmed around their huge cocks, the scents and sounds started to fade, like I was walking through fog, slipping away until they were—gone.

I was alone. Empty.

My pussy clenching and pulsing around nothing.

I tried to curl into a ball, but couldn't move.

I drifted back to reality slowly, requiring several minutes to emerge from a strange daze, to discover that I was strapped to a medical examination table in Earth's processing unit for the Interstellar Bride Program. I blinked, returning to myself, and to the woman I'd spent too much time with the last few days.

Warden Egara stared down at me with dark eyes and a program tablet in her hand. My body trembled with continued need as aftershocks of the orgasm still fluttered through my pussy. The exam table was cold and the gown I wore was open in the back. The standard gray cloth was covered with small replicas of the Interstellar Bride Program's insignia in a repeating pattern of red. I felt like I was wearing wallpaper.

"Very good, Hannah. The matching process is complete." Warden Egara was a stern-faced young woman who took her job, matching human women to their alien mates, very seriously. She looked at the medical equipment on the wall above my head and nodded to an assistant in a plain gray uniform who entered the room and began to remove the wires, tubes, and sensors they had attached to my head and body for the match assessment.

"What was that, a dream?" I licked my lips, parched from crying out my release. I wanted to know. A dream? A fantasy? Some deep, dark need I had buried so long ago that I didn't even know it existed? I'd just dreamt of being spanked and fucked, and not just by one man, but two. I'd also come harder than I ever had in my life.

"Oh, no, dear," the warden commented. "That was the recorded mating ritual of another human bride. That recording is several years old and belonged to a bride I sent there in the early days of the program." Warden Egara's face held a hint of a smile, the first I'd seen from her since entering the building for processing several days ago. She was very dedicated to her job. Very thoughtful, as if she had a personal interest in the happiness of every unmated warrior in the galaxy.

"You mean… I? That was… what?" What was I trying to say? "That was real?"

"Oh, yes. The Neuroprocessing Units used by the

matching system will be embedded in your body during final processing for transport. Not only does the NPU help you understand and speak their language, it has been preprogrammed to record your own mating ceremony so it can be properly documented and used to assist other brides in their own matching. Just like the other woman's experience was used to help match you."

I shuddered and wished she'd left me there, in that dreamland, for a few more minutes. I wanted more. Craved it. "Will my mate be like that?" Like what, I wasn't sure. I never got to see a face, but I knew. I *knew* I wanted him. Or them.

But two men? That was why I was confused.

"There were two men. Was I matched to two men?"

She shook her head. "No. You are only matched to one male. And your primary mate will be a warrior, but it will not be *that* warrior."

What did *primary mate* mean?

I shuddered and tried to imagine what might happen to me in the future. Would my mate be as big? As strong? Would I feel what that other bride felt? Would my mate want to include a second man in our mating ceremony? Would I want him to? What I had just experienced had gone beyond eagerness to total trust. Raw, mindless lust. Would I be as happy to be claimed as she had been?

I had never imagined being spanked before. I'd only thought of it as punishment, so I never would have volunteered for *that*. Truth be told, I didn't want to be matched to an alien mate at all. But, here I was, strapped to this freaking table in the processing center and it was my own fault. I'd volunteered for the Interstellar Bride Program to help get my brother out of debt with some very nasty people. He had three kids and a wife and if he didn't come up with a large sum of cash, they were all going to be on the streets. Or worse. Much worse.

My job as a preschool teacher barely paid me enough to survive on my own. I didn't have any extra money to give my brother. But I could do this.

Until this moment, I hadn't really believed there would be anything enjoyable in the matching process for me. I had doubted the bride program's ability to find a suitable match. I mean, really? How could a stupid computer program know which man in the entire galaxy would be perfect for me? I'd never found the right guy on Earth, so how could they find an alien match for me on a distant planet? The quivering pleasure I'd just experienced made me hopeful. *Very* hopeful. It was the first time in the past few weeks that I'd felt *maybe* things would be all right. Maybe volunteering for the Interstellar Bride Program hadn't been the biggest mistake of my life.

Mistake or not, family was family. This was the only way I could help my brother. My body and my life were all I had left of value. I wasn't rich, but I was young and fertile and unattached. Hell, uninspired was more like it. I'd had three lovers in five years, and none of them had made me come as hard as I just had… from a neural simulation. From another woman's memories.

Oh, God. I wanted one of those big, deep voices behind me. I wanted a huge hand wrapped and resting on my throat with a hot tongue stroking my clit. I wanted to be held in place as someone fucked me from behind. *I wanted…*

My monitor beeped and I blushed, knowing it was reading the increase in my heart rate as I relived everything that had just happened to me. No, it hadn't happened to me, but to her. The other woman. The one Warden Egara had sent to Prillon. The one who had been claimed by a warrior. A big, strong warrior with a huge cock. Her *primary mate.* Whatever that meant.

"So, is that where I've been matched? To that woman's planet?"

Warden Egara nodded curtly. "Yes. To a warrior of Prillon Prime."

Prillon Prime? I'd been matched to Prillon Prime? The planet inhabited by the hulking warrior race? The program's

GRACE GOODWIN

brochures had said that Prillon warriors actually requested brides while still in active military service. They were one of only three races that kept their brides with them on battleships. In space. On the front lines of the war between the biological races and the Hive, the artificial lifeforms and cyborg races trying to take over the universe. That war had finally come to Earth, and the coalition had accepted Earth under their protection, on one very strict condition.

Brides. A thousand a year. Most of Earth's brides came from the criminal justice system. Earth's politicians were not opposed to sacrificing *criminals* to fill the alien bride quota, but here I was, a volunteer hoping I hadn't just made the biggest mistake of my life.

I remembered reading that the Prillon males were supremely confident in their warriors' abilities to care for their mates. Anywhere. Prillon warriors never shied away from battle and were the most feared race in the Interstellar Coalition. They were on the front lines of the war, and their commanders were in charge of the entire interstellar fleet.

Holy shit. I wasn't going to a planet! I was going to go live on a spaceship in the middle of nowhere where they actually fought other spaceships? Or cyborgs. Or whatever! The heart rate monitor began beeping once again and this time it wasn't arousal I was feeling. It was panic.

I shook my head. Once, twice. "No. There must be some mistake."

"No mistake." She scowled at me. "Your match is estimated at ninety-nine percent compatibility."

"But…" I wanted to go to Forsia, or to the twin worlds of Ania and Axion, where they lived in cities surrounded by restaurants, parties, and opulence. I didn't want to go to a warship in *space*.

"Quiet." The word was bitten off as she hissed at me like an irritated cat. "It is done, the match complete. You already signed. Your family has been compensated, as you requested. Unless you wish to return the funds, you will honor your legal obligation to the program. You chose the

10

matching protocol. You must abide by the results."

Warden Egara was nice enough, in her twenties and even pretty, if a bit brusque. I understood. The woman at the front desk told me that they didn't get many volunteers. Most of the women Warden Egara processed were convicted criminals whose only two choices were either enter the Interstellar Bride Program or serve hard time in prison.

"Hmm. I believe I will add this outburst to your bride data. Your new mate should be warned of your impertinence."

My eyes widened and my mouth fell open.

"Just a minute! I never agreed to that." Impatient, I yanked at a couple of sticky pads attached to my temples and grimaced as they snagged on my long black hair. I handed them to the assistant, who finished unhooking me from the rest of it and left the room. Warden Egara must have realized that I was about to shove that tablet up her ass, for she held out her hand in a placating gesture.

"All right, Miss Johnson. I will delete that from your profile." She tapped the screen again and frowned. Her long hair was pulled into a tight bun and the strain on her skin made her look even more severe. "Now, for the record, state your name."

I took a deep breath, let it out. "Hannah Johnson."

"Miss Johnson, are you now, or have you ever been married?"

"No."

"Do you have any biological offspring?"

"No." I rolled my eyes. They'd already asked me this. I'd signed this shit in triplicate and I was sure it was listed on her tablet.

"Excellent." She tapped her screen a few times without looking at me. "I am required to inform you, Miss Johnson, that you will have thirty days to accept or reject the mate chosen for you by our matching protocols." She lifted her head and actually grinned at me. "Judging by these scores, however, I think that is highly unlikely."

I wasn't as confident in the computer program they used to match brides to their mates, but I was reassured that the ultimate decision was mine. "Okay."

"Regardless of your choice, there will be no return to Earth. If your new mate is unacceptable, you may request a new primary mate after thirty days… on Prillon Prime. You may continue this process until you find a mate who is acceptable."

"Warden, I just want to know…"

She sighed. "You have already signed the documents, Miss Johnson, but I also feel obligated to remind you that as of this moment, you are no longer a citizen of Earth, but a warrior bride of Prillon Prime, and, as such, you shall be bound by the laws and customs of your new world."

"But—"

"You have been matched, Hannah, to one of the fiercest warriors from that world. You should be proud. Serve him well." I wasn't sure if Warden Egara's command was meant to encourage me or frighten me, but I didn't have long to wonder. I had no idea that she knew anything personal about the alien males she matched. Apparently, she knew more than I did. Perhaps she liked me more than I imagined. If I were a crazy serial killer, would she still send me to this fierce warrior? Did she tell all women some lie about how fantastic their match was to make them eager to leave Earth?

She stepped forward and shoved on the side of my medical chair. With a small jolt, a bright blue opening appeared in the side of the wall. Still strapped securely, I could do nothing as a long, very large needle appeared. The needle was attached to a long metallic arm in the wall. I tried to pull back and she raised her voice so I could hear her over the bubbling of the strange blue liquid below me.

"Do not fight it, Hannah. That device will simply implant your permanent NPUs. Nothing to fear." Her smile was forced and her lips thin, but at least she was trying to reassure me. I got the feeling she didn't do this kind of warm and fuzzy thing often.

I slid into the tiny enclosure and felt the sting of the needle first on one side of my temple, then the other. I was quite sure that the strange and very strong buzzing sensation I now felt on both sides of my head would give me a migraine from hell. Resigned to suffer the effects of the NPU, I was lowered into a heated bath of some sort. Blue light surrounded me.

"When you wake, Hannah Johnson, your body will have been prepared for Prillon Prime's matching customs and your mate's requirements. He will be waiting for you."

Holy shit. "Now? Right now?" I struggled against the cuffs that held my wrists to the table. "I haven't even said goodbye to my brother! Wait!"

For some reason, my anger and frustration just disappeared, as if the warm bath washed it away. What the heck was in the water? I felt so relaxed, so happy.

So numb.

Warden Egara's clipped voice was the last thing I heard above the quiet humming of electrical equipment and lights. "Your processing will begin in three… two… one…"

Everything faded to black.

CHAPTER TWO

Commander Zane Deston, Prillon Warship, Sector 764

The bitter taste of protocol weighed down my tongue as I listened to the warriors gathered around the table. We were lucky enough to have soundly defeated the enemy, the Hive, in this sector more than a month ago, and unlucky enough to now have the honor of hosting Prillon Prime's heir, Prince Nial, on board my warship. The young prince was to be mated when he returned to our home world, and he was delaying the inevitable for as long as possible. He was a highly skilled pilot, but he was untested. He wanted a taste of combat, not the pampered palace existence he'd experienced his entire life.

The Battleship Deston, named after its commander, was the only place in the universe he could hide from the Prime, his father, the king of our world. This ship was the only place immune from the Prime's powerful reach.

This ship was *mine*. As a commander with royal blood, not even the royal house could take it from me. Not only was I the Prime's cousin, but I'd proven myself in many battles. Allies and enemies alike whispered my name in fear.

Despite my reputation across the entire interstellar fleet, I was forced to remain in this sector. Waiting. A woman, my new mate, the mate I didn't want or need here screwing up my life or my routines, was to be transported and we had to remain stationary to receive her. I hadn't even made the request of the Interstellar Bride Program myself. My mother had done that without my knowledge or permission. I'd been forced to accept a bride and name a second. If I had refused, I would have dishonored my entire family.

The fact that my mate was unwanted was my secret, my burden to bear. The crew aboard my warship was happy for the delay in our return to the frontier, and eager to meet their new matriarch. My second, Dare, was eager to claim a female and share her with me as true warriors did. Both the primary and secondary males shared the pleasures and responsibilities of the female and her offspring. We lost too many warriors in battle and the custom of sharing a mate ensured that no mated female was ever left all alone. Two warriors from a family line were pledged to every female's life, body, and honor. If one died, a new second was named.

I had named my second. I had participated in the matching process. And now all I could do was pretend to be pleased at the match and accept whatever bride was sent to me. I simply hoped she would be intelligent enough not to be a hindrance, and strong enough to accept my nature. Prillon brides were rare, and powerful in their own right. My bride would wield much power, if she were worthy enough for me to give it to her. I wanted a mate who would submit to my every need, but my very base, dominant needs had frightened more than one female from my world. I couldn't imagine a fragile female from Earth would fare better. I knew I would need to maintain control of myself, keep my true nature contained, if I didn't want a terrified bride.

"I'm sure your bride will arrive any time, commander. The transport was to be initiated today."

"I'm sure her hair will be like spun gold and her eyes a dark shade of amber." Harbart spoke from his place of honor standing at Prince Nial's right shoulder. Harbart was a pompous little ass, a stooped old man and a creature devoted not to the sacred act of war, but to the distasteful duties of politics, in particular the rise of his daughter as Prince Nial's betrothed.

Thank the gods for that. If not for Harbart's interest in my cousin, Nial, the poisonous old man would have most likely set his sights on mating his daughter to me. Currently, I was third in line to the throne. I needed Nial to claim a bride and start producing offspring as quickly as possible.

"Thank you, Harbart." I accepted his good wishes and leaned back in my command chair. The table in the meeting room seated six of my captains—all formidable warriors with the dark golden hair and yellow eyes common to our people—and the prince. For three hours we had reviewed reports and battle preparations. All ship sections had reported in. All repairs had been made after our last battle with the Hive. Now, an entire battle group, five thousand warriors and ten ships, were stranded in space waiting on a female. *My* female.

Dread filled my gut at the very idea.

Harbart opened his mouth to speak and I caught the gaze of my first officer, who rolled his eyes as the communications beacon dinged. My medical officer's voice filled the small meeting room. "Commander, we have taken your mate to medical station one. She arrived a few minutes ago, unconscious, but stable."

Regardless of my disinterest in a bride, I was curious about the woman matched to me. Every muscle in my body went taut with the need to rush to the medical section and inspect her. I could not do so, not now. If I did, every male in the room would demand to accompany me. I would rot in the tar pits on Prillon Prime before I allowed the sniveling politician, Harbart, to see my bride's naked form. I might not have requested the woman, but that did not make her any less *mine*. Mine to see, mine to care for, and mine to fuck.

The claiming ceremony was sacred and private; only my closest warriors, those I trusted with both my life and hers, would be allowed to bear witness to the claiming. In bearing witness, they vowed to honor and protect my new mate as a sacred part of me, as half of my body, half of my flesh. They pledged their lives to her protection. And before that ceremony could begin, I needed to ensure she accepted me and my second, and that she was committed to our match. Prillon brides were never forced to accept a mate. I frowned. If I couldn't tame my new bride in the next thirty days without scaring her away, I didn't deserve to keep her.

Regardless of the timing, I'd slit Harbart's throat before I allowed him to witness that blessed rite.

"Very well, doctor," I replied, my voice calm and even. "No one is to see her but me. I will come to her after my meeting with the engineers."

"Yes, commander."

The communication unit went quiet and so did the room as the men stared at me in disbelief.

"Why do you not rush to her side, commander?" Harbart's outraged question confirmed that I had made the correct decision. The vile male couldn't wait to set his lecherous eyes on my mate.

His obvious jealousy made possessiveness flare. To my surprise, desire for an unseen woman heated my blood and I fought back the urge to rush to her, to see her, to taste her flesh and claim her body with my own. She was matched to me out of every other male in the universe. Her desires were matched to mine and I was eager to test the program's success. Perhaps my mother had been right to force the issue. Knowing my mate was onboard the ship caused my mind to shift. Logic insisted I did not require a bride, but with her so near, my body had other ideas.

Her arrival would be known throughout the battle group in a matter of hours and the ship would be a dangerous place for my new mate until I claimed her, especially with Harbart's royal entourage aboard. Stealing females had once been very common on Prillon Prime, and some old fools, like Harbart, longed for the days when men took their brides by the strength of their sword or their armies.

Fools. Many fine warriors had died at the hands of their new brides before the archaic laws had been changed by the current Prime, killed by brides angry and savaged by the loss of their chosen mates. Even now, I refused to jeopardize my bride by showing too much interest. The more I valued her, the bigger target she would be for calculating and power-hungry bastards like Harbart. He was not the only elder or the only politician onboard my ship. They could all rot, as far as I was concerned.

"I will not neglect my duties or become distracted by a mate." I rose from my seat and the warriors under my command followed suit, all but Prince Nial. My cousin grinned up at me.

"We'll see about that, cousin."

With a scowl, I stared back at him. "You will go on the next scout run with Dare, cousin. Try not to get yourself killed." Dare was my second and my best combat pilot. I didn't trust the prince's safety to any other.

Nial grinned. Harbart blustered protests, and I exited the meeting room and walked onto the command deck of my ship, already issuing new orders to my navigator. "Now that the transport is complete, there will be no more waiting. Alert the captains. Prepare for departure. We leave for the front within the hour."

"Yes, commander."

I left the command deck and made my way straight to the ship's engine rooms for my scheduled meeting with the engineers. I did my best to listen, but all I could think about was the female waiting for me in the medical bay.

What would she be like? Would she tremble in fear at first sight of me, as so many females did on my home world? Would she bow and avert her eyes in deference to my battle prowess and superior rank? Would she dare defy me, or would she submit to my will in all things? Would she be soft and curved with large breasts like the women programmed into the ship's pleasure simulators or would she be lean and strong, like the warrior women from my home world?

The third time I was forced to ask the engine mechanic to repeat himself, I ended the meeting. I was tired of waiting.

The medical deck was not far, and within minutes I stormed into the space expecting to find my bride awake and waiting for me.

Instead, the doctor hurried to my side with a concerned slant to his brow.

"Commander, she has not yet regained consciousness."

My chest constricted with an unfamiliar ache and I scowled at the man. "Why not?"

"I don't know. All of her scans appear to be normal. Her name is Hannah Johnson. She is from a place called North America. And this is interesting, commander, she is the first volunteer I have seen from Earth. Most brides from that planet are criminals."

Doctor Mordin held his monitoring tablet out for my inspection, but I didn't care to read about her on a machine, nor did I care where she came from. I had been in many battles with Mordin, and counted him a trusted friend. If anything were seriously wrong with my mate, he would have informed me already. I did not care what the bureaucrats in the Interstellar Bride Program had put on their ridiculous forms. She was mine now, she was here, and I wanted to see her in the flesh.

"Take me to her."

"Of course." He turned and went into a private suite normally reserved for visiting royalty or high-ranking officers. It was the only private bay in the medical station, and I was thankful for his discretion.

I stood in the doorway as he hurried to my bride's bedside with his scanners. Arms crossed, I allowed him to finish his scans. I could not see much of her, for the man blocked my view. Despite the fact that I now had a mate only due to my mother's interference, I discovered that since she had arrived, I was very... interested. Eager, even.

"Is she well?"

"She appears unharmed, but I can't perform a full breeding diagnostic until she is awake."

"Has anyone come to inquire after her?"

The doctor's smirk was pure malice, and I was grateful to call him a loyal and trusted friend. He was not just trained to heal, but to kill, and was a fierce warrior. "Oh, the prince's puppet was here, but I turned him away."

Fury pumped through my veins. "Excellent. Thank you."

He nodded once. "My honor, commander."

"Leave us."

He grinned. "Of course."

I waited for the door to slide closed behind him before turning to the small bed on which my bride slumbered.

I expected golden hair and amber eyes. But my mate's hair was long, straight, and black as night with shimmering strands that looked soft to touch. Unusual, but beautiful beyond reckoning. Equally dark eyebrows arched over delicate eyes, and black lashes rested on pale cheeks. Her skin was the palest I'd ever seen, much fairer than my darker coloring. I couldn't miss her full pink lips or the hint of blush on her cheeks.

I longed to see her eyes, to discover if they were as exotic as her dark hair and smooth skin.

She was covered by a sheet and I gently tugged it away to inspect the rest of her. Her naked body was lush and curved, her breasts large with enticing dusky rose nipples. Any hair she may have had on her body had been removed, as was our custom, leaving her flesh bare and smooth.

My cock stirred to life, rising in greeting and ready to claim what was mine. She was so small, so tiny in comparison to me and my second. This was not right! The Interstellar Bride Program must have made a mistake.

I swallowed down a surge of disappointment at her size. I would need to be careful with her. Gentle. As commander, I was in charge of this battleship and a whole fleet of others.

I had power and control that I wielded with firm command. I wanted to be free to wield that same intensity of power over her body. Looking at her, I realized for the first time that I needed that release and more from my new mate. But she was not from Prillon, and was so small that I imagined my full pleasure would surely hurt her.

So I would be careful. Tender. Remaining constantly aware of her size and small body.

I draped the sheet back over her. I wanted her, but I would not take her like this. I wanted to watch as her eyes widened when my cock filled her the first time, to hear her moans of pleasure as I made her come. I could control my dominant urges and still fuck her. I would seek pleasure from her body—often—and she would know that my second and I were the ones to give it to her.

Leaning over her, I tucked the sheet around her shoulders. Glancing up, I discovered a pair of eyes gazing at me, the irises a deep brown so dark they were nearly indistinguishable from the center.

My heart skipped a beat. A fierce warrior, I shouldn't have such a visceral response to a small female. I froze, not wanting to scare her. I didn't know how men on Earth were sized, but I was of great size for a Prillon warrior. Awake, she seemed even smaller and more fragile, striking, and extraordinary.

"Where am I?" She stared at me but didn't panic or attempt to run. Her voice was melodic and beautiful, and it did not waver or shake with fear. Very reassuring.

"You are on board a Prillon battleship, in the medical station."

That made her eyes go wide and she struggled to sit up until her back rested against the wall, clutching the sheet to her chest. "Medical station? I'm on a spaceship? You're a doctor? Oh, my God. Is he here?"

"Who?" I sat down on the edge of her bed and was thrilled when she didn't move away. I wanted to touch her. Everywhere. Now that she was awake, I wanted to explore her, discover if her body was as soft as it looked. I wondered how she tasted, if her nipples would harden beneath my Prillon tongue, if her pussy tasted as sweet as I hoped.

"My match? Warden Egara said my mate was one of the fiercest warriors of Prillon Prime." Her gaze locked with mine and her eyes widened.

"He is." My chest swelled with pride. So, my battle prowess had reached ears as far away as the new planet under coalition protection, Earth.

"Is he… big like you?" She licked her lips and I stifled a groan. I knew she wasn't referring to my cock, but that was the direction of my thoughts. My cock was… big, as she would soon discover.

My eyes wandered over her face, down the long line of her pale neck. "Yes. He looks like me. Do you find me offensive to the eye?"

I waited patiently as she inspected the hard angles of my face and jaw. I wasn't blue or green, as were some males from the other coalition planets, but perhaps different from men on her world.

"May I see your hands?" she asked.

Curious, I held my hands in front of her and watched her face turn from pale to pink. She reached toward me tentatively, but drew back before making contact. My hands were easily twice the size of hers, but I craved to feel her hesitant touch.

An odd pink coloration of her skin rushed from her shoulders up her neck to her cheeks.

"Why does looking at my hands make your skin change color?"

"What?" She startled and tore her gaze from my hands to look up at me. "It's nothing. Just—I was remembering something." She held the sheet in place under her arms and lifted her fingertips to explore the sides of her head where I noticed thin scars rested on both temples.

"Are you in pain? Are the neural implants causing you discomfort?"

22

If my bride was hurting, I'd have the doctor back in here immediately. I took care of what was mine, and I discovered an unexpected but instinctive need to protect and care for the small human female before me. I would need to protect her, even from myself.

"No. Not really. It feels like a quiet buzzing in my head." She frowned and pressed her fingertips to her skin, tracing the edges of the thin implants permanently embedded in her skull. "But I understand you, so I guess they're working."

Every member of the Interstellar Coalition's military had the implants. They were programmed for language and assisted the brain with advanced computations. The implants were vital to our fleet and allowed for ease of communication and understanding between the over two hundred member planets of the coalition.

She dropped her hands to the bed beside her and looked up at me. "When will I meet him?"

"Very soon. Are you afraid?"

She bit her lip. "A little." Her gaze wandered over my face, lingering on my eyes and the sharp lines of my cheekbones.

"Do I look so different from Earth men?" I wondered.

She sighed. "No. Not really. You're much bigger and your face has harsher angles." She lifted a hand toward me, as if to explore the shape of my face, but dropped it to her lap before making contact. Why was she so fearful of touching me? Ah yes, she didn't know I was her mate.

"Your skin is a bit different. Darker, as if you've been out in the sun."

"You are the one whose skin changes color," I replied.

I watched as her pale flesh changed color again.

"That's blushing. I do it... when nervous or embarrassed."

"Ah." That was a reasonable bodily response and something that would help me learn my mate's moods. "What happens when you are aroused?"

She... blushed an even more delightful shade of pink.

"I—"

The words died in her throat as our gazes locked and I could no longer hide my need to touch her. She wrapped her arms across her breasts in alarm. "You're him, aren't you? You're my mate."

"Yes, Hannah Johnson of Earth. I am Commander Zane Deston. You are mine." I leaned over and took her small hands in my own, holding them in place on her lap as I closed the distance between us. The doctor would return soon, but my need for her overcame my restraint. I would wait no longer. "And I will taste you now."

CHAPTER THREE

Hannah

My new mate was huge, bigger than any Earth man I'd ever dated, close to seven feet tall with massive shoulders and thighs. He wore a dense brown and black armor covered in a camouflage pattern similar to what the military used on Earth. He didn't look the least bit soft. His eyes were dark amber and were startling in his face. The angles of his cheeks, nose, and jaw were perhaps a bit sharper than a human's, but oddly handsome. His gaze was focused and intense, and I saw lust there, raw and untamed, and my nipples hardened under the sheet as his big hands covered mine. This magnificent male was mine. Mine! He looked like what he was, a predator. A warrior.

Someone who could keep me safe.

My hands were trapped in my lap, held easily in place by my new mate's firm grip as he leaned in close to *taste* me. I wasn't sure exactly what that meant until his lips landed on mine and his long, rough tongue invaded my mouth.

His kiss—Zane's kiss—was not like those of the boys I'd kissed on Earth. He pressed my head to the wall and demanded a response, holding me still as he plundered and explored my mouth. His kiss stole my air and my reason as his oddly long tongue wrapped completely around mine and tugged gently.

I could just imagine that length inside my pussy, teasing my g-spot until I screamed, or roughly vibrating as he licked my clit. I could imagine the coarse fibers lapping and suckling my nipples as his cock filled me to the brink of pain and his large hands held me in place, unable to move, unable to resist.

My whole body felt like a live wire, hyper-alert and so aware of my mate that I could barely breathe. His kiss melted my resistance and I didn't try to struggle or fight his hold on me. Instead I welcomed the aggressive push of his tongue in my mouth and the steel-like grip of his hands on mine. My pussy clenched and fluttered with heat and the wet evidence of my arousal quickly coated my thighs. Memories flooded me with the exotic scent of his skin, and my body responded as if I was still in the bride program's matching simulator, experiencing the touch of another warrior.

He could take me right here, right now, and I wasn't sure I had the will to stop him. This warrior was mine. Mine. *Mine.*

I couldn't hold back the soft moan that left my throat any more than I could tell my heart to stop racing like a wild thing behind my ribs. His tasting went on and on until I was panting and limp in his arms.

This was my mate, my match, the *one man* in the universe who was supposed to be perfect for me. Everything feminine within me wanted to surrender to him, to just let go and allow someone else to take care of me for once in my life. I'd had the urge to submit before and with disastrous results. My last boyfriend on Earth had taken advantage of me, used me and never really cared. He had made so many promises with his alpha male attitude and his sexual domination that I'd given in and trusted him. I'd been betrayed by this weakness I had for aggressive men who took and took and took until they broke me.

I tore my mouth from his, afraid of him, of his instant power over me, and even more, afraid of myself. I knew nothing about him. How could I trust him so quickly? It was stupid and weak, match or not. The computer program at the bride processing center said this male, this alien, was the perfect man for me. Almost a 100% certainty of it. But what if it was wrong? What if he'd lied on his application to the program or turned out to be a user like all the rest of the men in my life? Even my own brother had used me in the end. He'd been perfectly happy to let me sacrifice myself and become an interstellar bride because it meant he didn't have to work off his own debt or pay for his own mistakes. I'd done it anyway, not for him, but for my three nieces. Without the money I was able to give them, they would most likely have been taken and sold by the dark underworld criminals who held my idiot brother's debt.

I tried to slow my rapid breathing, my frantic heart. Even the scent of him, something almost woodsy, taunted me. No. *No!* Men were not to be trusted. Neither was my body, apparently. It turned traitor so quickly, wanting to surrender to this big alien and give him complete control as I angled my head without thought.

"Stop." I could barely get the word out, but he froze, his mouth tracing the curve of my neck, that rough tongue tasting me like I was his new favorite treat. My skin tingled everywhere he tasted. I clenched my fists beneath his as I fought my own body.

He growled with displeasure and pulled back to look me in the eye. "You cannot lie to me, mate. I smell the sweet honey between your legs. I can hear your heart racing and see the flutter of your pulse in your neck. You want this." He leaned forward to claim my mouth again, his lips hovering just over mine. "You want me to fill you up and make you mine forever."

His gravelly voice made me squirm with lust, but he'd loosened his hold on my hands and I hurriedly reached up to cover my lips with my fingertips before he could make contact. "I barely know your name."

With a sigh, he leaned back to sit straight on the bed again and I breathed a sigh of relief.

"True, my wise little one. Your brain only knows my name, but your body knows so much more." His brow winged up. "You will deny that is true, but your body tells me otherwise. As commander, this warship is mine. I am called Commander Deston, but you, mate, and only you, may call me Zane."

"All right. My name is Hannah. We don't use our second names on Earth, unless it's for something legal, or a formality."

Zane nodded and I tried to smile, tried to relax. At least he wasn't pushing himself on me—even if, perhaps, I wanted that kiss to continue. There was time for that... later, but I had some basic questions. I glanced around the room, but it only looked like a hospital room on Earth. Nothing space-like. "We're really in outer space?"

"Yes. We have been waiting for your arrival before returning to the front. Now that you are safely on board, we will rejoin the others in battle."

All the heat that had flooded my body drained from me instantly. The front? Warship? Battle? I knew Prillon brides were kept on battleships. I knew it before I was sent here. But the reality of being trapped on a ship during a real battle, where things blew up and people died, was suddenly terrifying. No longer abstract. Dangerous and scary and real. "I can't go into battle. They must have made a mistake with my match. I have to go home." I tried to shift and climb off the bed, but I realized I wasn't going anywhere with Zane's large body blocking my way. I also remembered I was naked under the sheet.

He scowled, and the expression turned his features into those of a predator. Scared now, I felt my eyes grow wide as I tried to back away from him. That seemed to anger him even more and his gaze darkened and his nostrils flared. "You aren't going anywhere, nor shall you speak of leaving me again. I have tasted your desire, Hannah. We are very compatible."

"But battle…?"

"You are afraid," he commented, his eyes watching me carefully.

"Of course I'm afraid! We're in a ship in the middle of space, in the middle of a war. I don't want to die." My heart pounded against my chest and I struggled in Zane's hold, the bitter taste of panic flooding my mouth.

"Silence." He raised a hand. "You are perfectly safe, Hannah. This is a Prillon battleship. My battleship. We have never lost a battle, little one. Do not question my ability to protect you."

I shook my head, suddenly recalling every sci-fi movie battle scene in my mind. "What if the ship crashes? Or blows up? What if your ship gets boarded by aliens and they take prisoners? What if I get transported onto another ship? Or taken by your enemies? What if you get killed and some other man tries to claim me?"

"I am *your* mate and you will not have another. There is no place safer—no *one* safer to be with than me. Your mate. And you need not worry about being alone. I have named a second, as our custom demands. You will always be cared for and protected. Always." While he stroked a finger down my cheek, he added, "I have been too soft with you. I understand now why the protocols for claiming a bride were written. I shall not break them again, nor give you an excuse to choose another." He took my chin and tilted it up with his thumb. I couldn't help but meet his amber gaze. "Forgive me, mate. I will see to your care now, as I should have from the beginning. I will not fail you again."

For some reason, his mercurial mood swings, from sexually aggressive, to anger, to this tenderness, made my eyes burn. What the heck was wrong with me? Was it the possibility of imminent death? Was it the transport? Had it scrambled my brain? I had no idea what to say, so I simply nodded.

"Good girl." He stood and I immediately missed the warmth of his leg pressed to my thigh through the sheet. When his back was turned, I licked my lips, where his exotic taste lingered around my mouth.

He strode to the door with purpose, waited for it to slide open and nodded to someone I could not see. He turned around and another male followed him back into the room. They looked similar, but the other Prillon warrior had dark gray eyes. He did not wear the mottled armor that Zane wore, but a deep green with an odd symbol on his chest that I did not recognize.

"This is Doctor Mordin. He will complete your examination now."

I froze and held the sheet tightly to my chest. "I had a complete examination on Earth. I don't need another one. They confirmed my health. Surely, they sent you a report."

Zane crossed his arms and raised an eyebrow. "Hannah, you will obey me in this and allow the doctor to complete your examination. I must care for you, and you traveled through three transport centers to reach me. I will not neglect your health."

"You said we are headed for battle. Shouldn't you be focusing on more important things? Like cleaning your ray guns, or something?"

He took a step closer so I had to tilt my head back. "I do not know what a ray gun is, but it does not matter, mate. There is *nothing* more important than you."

"But... but I'm fine. I—" Words failed me when Zane growled.

"Do you refuse to obey?" Zane's tone was harsh but the doctor, I could see, was hiding a grin behind whatever odd devices he had carried into the room.

Obey? I could tell that the mighty *Commander* Deston wasn't used to being disobeyed, but I didn't want another stupid alien touching me right now, even if he was a doctor. "I don't need an exam."

"You are acting like a spoiled child."

30

My mouth fell open. "No, I'm not."

"I can see that you will need a lesson in Prillon discipline, little one. I had assumed the rules of your submission would have been included as part of your preparations for transport, just as your body was prepared according to our customs."

Prepared? I frowned and pulled the sheet away from my body and glanced down. I… I had no hair between my legs. None at all. I rubbed my thighs together and it felt… smooth. God, what else had they done to *prepare* me?

"This must be corrected immediately. Instead of *knowing* what is expected and obeying, you will be *shown* what happens when you don't. You are my mate and as commander of this ship, I must set the example for my warriors. I will not tolerate a disobedient mate."

What the—

He crossed the room in two steps and ripped the sheet from my fingers. I screeched, but his stoic face was cold and hard as ice, and completely unmoved. Before I could even think about scrambling off the bed, he reached for me. Without any effort at all I'd been lifted, turned, and then resettled face down over his lap with both legs trapped beneath his left thigh, my stomach pressed into his right, and my bare bottom sticking up in the air like a naughty girl waiting to be—

Whoa. Where had that thought come from?

"What are you doing? Let me go right now!" I was mortified. The doctor stood behind me, with a clear view of my ass and pussy. Zane's legs trapped mine with the force of an unmovable mountain, and his right arm was pressed to my bare back, holding me down.

"You will not disobey me, mate. I cannot allow you to disregard your own health. Nor can I have you running around the ship disrespecting me in front of my crew."

"All right. I see that you are serious about this. I'm sorry. Just let me up."

His answer was a loud smack on my right cheek. It hurt.

He was spanking me! "Ow! This is bullshit. Let me—"

Smack.

The left cheek now stung too and I could feel my face getting red. Rage fueled me as he struck me again and again in a steady rhythm that caused my bare bottom to go from stinging pain with each strike to a constant burn.

To my horror, the burn spread through my body, making me squirm, not with rage, but with a craving for physical contact, for more sensory input, for more. My nipples hardened and my body felt like it was about to overload with sensation as he changed tactics, no longer striking me, but rubbing his huge, warm palm over my tender, heated flesh like he was petting his favorite kitten. So softly, so gently, as if I was precious and fragile. The complete shift made me feel upset and confused.

"Had you remained silent, I would be finished now, my mate. But you cursed at me, and no Prillon warrior's bride speaks to her mate in such a manner. You will obey me in all things. You will not demean yourself or disrespect yourself by allowing foul language to come from your perfect lips. You will care for yourself as if you were the most precious being alive on this ship, because to me, that's exactly what you are."

His caress calmed me, but his words made me even more uncomfortable than I had been before. I didn't examine the why, just renewed my struggles. I squirmed and shoved with my hands against the bed with all my might, but I might as well have been trying to push a boulder off my back. He wasn't hurting me, but I couldn't move.

"For your foul mouth, little one." He struck again, this time hitting the back of my tender thighs, where they met the curve of my bare bottom. The area was extremely sensitive and the sting of his large palm brought tears to my eyes. He continued spanking my thighs hard, not stopping until tears rolled down my face and I went limp in his arms. I was so confused, so hurt, and I didn't understand why he would do this to me.

When Zane finally freed my legs, I didn't try to move. I didn't know what to do. The stupid doctor was still there, watching everything and I felt lost. All I wanted to do was curl up in Zane's lap and have him pet me again and talk to me in that soft voice and make me feel like everything was going to be all right.

How could I want comfort from Zane when he was the reason I was so upset in the first place? I was losing my mind.

He rolled me over and repositioned me in his lap until I was exactly where I wanted to be, but never would have had the nerve to ask to be, safe and protected in his big, strong arms. I couldn't hold back my tears and he held me in silence as I cried, his hand gently rubbing up and down my bare back.

Several minutes passed before my crying turned to hiccups and sniffles. I stopped trying to figure out what was happening to me. I'd been transported halfway across the galaxy, left everything I knew behind and woke up to an alien who'd kissed me senseless, then spanked my bare bottom simply because I'd argued with him and used a curse word.

Now that I thought about the doctor bit, I guess it did make sense. If Zane had traveled across the galaxy to reach Earth, I'd want him to be checked out by a doctor there. I'd be worried about him because I cared. That made sense. Except, how could he care about me at all when we'd just met?

"Are you ready to let the doctor take a look at you? We need to make sure you are healthy and suffered no ill effects from your transport." His voice was gentle, but there was steel behind the words. I knew if I denied him again, I'd be right back over his lap getting another spanking.

"All right. Yes."

"Good girl."

Why did that praise make me happy? Why did I suddenly *want* to please him, a complete stranger? Oh, I knew that I'd always been susceptible to an alpha male, to the most basic and fundamental craving to have someone strong care for me and protect me. But I'd been burned by men before, more than once. And I barely knew Zane. Why was my body acting like it knew him, like it trusted him already? My body seemed to be developing a will of its own, and I wasn't sure I was in agreement with it.

"I'm going to lay you back down on the bed. Relax and let the doctor make sure everything is working properly." His tone was gentle and calm, as if the previous few minutes, his striking my bare ass, had never happened.

I nodded and wiped away the last of my tears as he stood with me in his arms. He squeezed me gently, as if I truly was precious to him, then turned and laid me down on my back. I wasn't settled at the head of the small bed where I had been before, but at the bottom with my bare ass literally hanging off the end. His arm held my legs in place as the doctor pulled two stirrups out from some mysterious hiding place. When the doctor nodded, Zane placed my feet in the stirrups and stepped back.

Shit. A gynecological exam? Now?

CHAPTER FOUR

Hannah

Stirrups. Ass hanging off the table. A stranger between my legs.

I knew this setup all too well. For a moment, I considered protesting, then stopped myself before I ended up back over his knee. My bottom and the backs of my thighs still stung from his very thorough spanking and I didn't want more.

I took a deep breath, let it out slowly. I'd been through this on Earth before, many times, hell, once a year since I'd turned sixteen. I could bear it if it would make the doctor happy, my mate happy, and get me the hell out of this stupid medical room.

The doctor stood between my legs with a clinically blank expression on his face, which helped. "I'll try to make this quick, Lady Hannah."

I met the man's gaze briefly, then looked up at the metal ceiling, noticed the rivets that held it in place. I refused to look at either man. "Fine."

Mortified, I laid back, placed my bent elbow over my eyes. My entire naked body was on display, and my pussy was hanging open and exposed off the end of the table in front of not just one, but two strange, alien men. To make it even worse, surely my bottom was red from the spanking Zane had given me.

I heard Zane move, but had no idea what he intended until he settled onto the bed above me, lifted my head and placed it in his lap. I uncovered my eyes to find him looking down at me. He ignored the doctor completely. "Give me your hand, mate."

I didn't realize how much I needed the reassurance until I lifted my left hand and placed it in his. He squeezed gently and suddenly I didn't feel so alone on this strange ship with alien warriors.

"Go ahead now, doctor. She is ready." He didn't take his eyes from mine as he spoke to the other man.

I ignored the warm hands at the tops of my thighs. I ignored the cold feel of medical lube that he smeared over my core. I even ignored the blunt tip of a cold, hard object as the doctor inserted it into my pussy. I expected the usual stretching of a speculum, but startled when the item was deep inside me, pressed up against my womb. I gasped at the feel of it.

"Hush, mate. It will be over soon." Zane's right hand came to rest on my shoulder, and as I watched, his eyes darkened with a look I already recognized on his strikingly handsome face. Lust.

"Ready, commander?" The doctor's question made me blink in confusion. Ready for what? Was it custom for the doctor to speak to Zane instead of me? I was the one naked, with my legs splayed wide and a thick, hard object filling my pussy.

"She is ready," he replied.

"What? I thought—" I gasped as a second object circled the rosy bud between the cheeks of my bare bottom. The doctor worked something small, perhaps no bigger around than a drink straw, into the tight hole and I felt a gushing wetness inside as some kind of warm liquid began to fill me. *There.*

Finally, after what seemed an eternity, he removed the small object and I realized I was panting and squeezing Zane's hand so hard I thought I might be hurting him. "What kind of exam is this? I don't think I was injured *there* during transport."

The men ignored me, and the doctor said, "Hold still, Lady Hannah. I don't want this to hurt."

With his warning ringing in my ears, I held completely still as he pressed something hard and cold to my virgin opening.

"Breathe, Hannah." Zane rubbed his hand along my right shoulder in a soothing gesture and I tried to listen to him as the doctor slowly pressed the object inside me. It stretched me, the tissues and untried muscles unused to the invasion. I moved my head from side to side as the pressure slowly continued.

"Zane, please," I gasped. "What is he doing?"

"You're doing well. Almost there." Doctor Mordin rubbed the inside of my thigh, as if to comfort me but I felt so humiliated, so damn naked. I had a huge device inside my pussy and now another, smaller one, inside my ass. I'd never felt this full, or stretched, or exposed.

I felt the object slide past my inner muscles and the burning lessened. I glanced down to see my bare pussy. I could see a long, dark object sticking out of me, but it was oddly built, with a hooked section that remained outside of me and curved upward. I wasn't sure what he'd put in my ass, but I could feel it. I clenched down on both hard objects.

God, could I feel it. I put my head back down on Zane's thigh and turned my head away to stare at the plain silver wall. I couldn't bear to look up into Zane's eyes, afraid he'd see the war going on inside me. I should be ashamed. I should be angry. I should be fighting this.

Instead, I felt my pussy grow wet as I ached for the doctor to move the hard object he'd shoved inside me. I wanted him to fuck me with it, pull it out and work it back

GRACE GOODWIN

into me while Zane watched. I wanted to lift my hips and beg the doctor to put his mouth on me while Zane held me down. This dark, needy part of me wanted to be pinned down and taken by both of them, just like in that simulation I'd gone through in the matching process. I wanted Zane's tongue on my breast and his hand over my throat as the doctor worked me with his devices and made me come.

Oh, God. What was wrong with me? Perhaps the men were both right to be worried and I'd been injured in the transfer. Surely I wouldn't think or feel like this otherwise.

I whimpered, so ashamed and humiliated and confused. I didn't know what to do and I didn't know how to deal with this dark revelation.

"Shhh," Zane soothed. "It's all right, Hannah. I will take care of you. No one will hurt you ever again. You have my word."

Zane's soft promise threatened to break my slender hold on control. If only I could believe him. If only I could trust him and tell him what my body needed, but I'd heard those words before. From a liar and a cheat, a man who used me to get to my—

"Ahh!" I arched up off the table as a strong suction was applied to my clit. Panting, I lifted my head to see the curved piece had been lowered and attached to my swollen nub. The suction device was attached to the black dildo by a long, flexible cord. The object both vibrated and applied suction to me at the same time and my body was on fire. I trembled as need built inside me, no matter how hard I fought against it.

What the fuck?

"This isn't a doctor's examination," I cried, trying to catch my breath. "This is wrong. So wrong. Zane!" I shouted for him to make it stop, but inside I begged for it to continue.

He held me down and leaned over me to answer. I could see nothing but his rugged face.

"We must test your nervous system's response to sexual

stimulation, mate. You need to let go, Hannah. You need to come for the doctor."

"What? Why?" I gasped as the object began to vibrate faster. Come for the doctor? Have an orgasm while he—

"Oh, God."

The doctor pulled the large, ribbed device from my pussy, then shoved it back inside me in one long, smooth glide. Again. And again. My hips rose from the table to meet his thrusts. I couldn't help it. I had no control over my own body. It had taken over. I was no longer Hannah Johnson of Earth. I was no one. I had no identity. I was just a body, a woman who needed to come.

"That's it, Hannah. Let go." Zane leaned over me and flicked his long tongue over my nipple just as the suction on my clit increased in strength. The doctor fucked me with the black device, the long cord attached to the suction device bending and flexing as he moved. The sensation on my clit never ceased and my body was strung as tight as a bowstring. I was on the edge and so scared I couldn't breathe. I couldn't do this. It was too strong. Too big for me to hold.

"No! It's too much. Zane… it's, oh, my God. I can't—" My head thrashed against his lap. Sweat broke out on my skin and I felt heated and flushed all over.

Zane's right hand slid down to my inner thigh and he pulled my leg out of the stirrup, spreading me wider, opening me to the doctor's attentions. I whimpered and lifted my free hand to his hair, tugging and pulling on him, holding onto him, my only anchor in this hurricane of sensation.

Zane lifted his lips from my nipple and kissed his way across my chest to the other side. "Do it, doctor."

"Yes, commander."

Those two words were my only warning as the doctor pumped the dildo into my pussy harder and faster with one hand, and shifted the object in my ass with the other. The sound of my desire, wet and slick, filled the small room. The machine attached to my clit sped up and Zane sucked hard on my neglected nipple.

My body came apart. I exploded, my nerves so overloaded that my entire body shook and I literally saw stars as my eyesight blurred into a temporary inky blackness. The spasms in my pussy went on and on, clenching around the doctor's fucking, squeezing the device he'd placed in my ass. I was so full that I came around them, stretched and helpless and out of control. Small spasms of hot pleasure made me clench around the devices over and over until I was wrung out and limp, until I had no will to raise my head from Zane's lap, let alone protest the pleasure I'd just experienced.

I floated back to reality slowly. Zane's gentle kisses felt like worship on my chest and shoulders as the doctor gently removed his equipment from my body. I hissed as the one in my ass stretched me wide, then slipped free. All at once I felt empty as I clenched down on... nothing.

The doctor left the room quietly, leaving me with my new mate and the hot sting of humiliation that made my face and throat burn. What the hell was wrong with me?

Tears streamed from the corners of my eyes, but I had no control or emotional attachment to them. It was as if my body was crying of its own accord from being so completely overwhelmed.

"Good, Hannah. Good." Zane wrapped me up in the sheet and pulled me into his lap just as the doctor came back in. The tender skin from the spanking heated and stung against the rough feel of Zane's thigh. I tensed and turned my head away until the doctor stood before me and placed a small box on the examination table next to us. My attention was diverted from it by something else he brought into the room with him. In his hand was a long black strand of some kind. It looked like a thick black satin ribbon.

"You have passed our medical requirements, Lady Hannah. The sensors read that your nervous system is functioning at optimal levels and you are healthy and fertile for breeding."

I wanted to say something sassy, like, *Gee, thanks so much*, but I held my tongue. My bottom was sore, inside and out, and I wanted to get as far away from the doctor as I could.

Both men remained silent and I finally lifted my head from Zane's chest to look at what the doctor held in front of me. "What is it?"

"You've earned the right to be a Prillon bride. Congratulations, Hannah. And welcome, my lady. Once you claim your place among us, we are all yours. All Prillon warriors will honor you, fight for you, and die to protect you."

I was so confused. I'd earned the right to be a Prillon bride because of a forced orgasm?

I stared at the object, which looked very much like a collar. I reached up and took it from the doctor's hand. "What do I do with it?"

"You place the band around your neck, and always display it. It is black now, Lady Hannah. But once you choose a mate, and accept his claim in the claiming ceremony, your band will take on the color of your mate's and expand to operate as a full Prillon body regulation system."

I did *not* want to know what that meant. Not right now. I couldn't take any more.

I looked up at Zane, just now noticing the deep red band around his neck. The collar was partially hidden by his armor. I looked away, unable to deal with any more new information. "Can we leave now? Please?"

He ran his hand down my arm. "I can't remove you from the sanctuary of the medical station until you place the band around your neck. Without it, you would be unprotected and any male could try to claim you."

"But, if it's black, that means I haven't chosen yet, so what's the difference?"

The doctor chuckled. "The difference, my lady, is that a black band means you are in an active claiming period with a mate and his second."

"I still don't understand what difference it makes if I haven't chosen."

"It means, Hannah, that I have chosen you." Zane's gaze locked with my own and the raw possession I saw in his eyes set hundreds of butterflies loose in my stomach. No man had ever looked at me like that, like I was the only thing in the universe that mattered. "If any male dares touch you or disrespects you in any way, I will challenge him to a death duel." Zane's soft growl made me feel cherished this time, and special, because I knew all that fire and primitive protective instincts were for me. His thumb traced my lower lip as he whispered to me, making a solemn vow. "Only my second and I will lay a single finger on your beautiful body, my Hannah. Anyone else? I will kill him."

Second? That had been mentioned several times but before I could ask after the term, the door to the room slid open. I stiffened as two more warriors entered. One was young, and quite handsome. The other looked to be an elder of their race, his face was lined and harsh, his skin color dull, not the golden tan look of Zane's. The cold expression on the elder's face as he looked at me made me want to climb around my mate and hide behind his very large, very formidable body. I tucked the sheet about me even tighter.

The old male spoke, and I tensed at his words. "Are we too late for the medical exam, commander? As Prince Nial's personal advisor and honored father to the future Prime, I was very much looking forward to sharing in the joys of the bride processing protocols." He squinted at me, and the look in his eyes was anything but friendly. It was clear he'd wanted to watch, all right. And not because he cared one bit about my health.

The tension in my mate's chest translated to my worn-out body and I began to tremble in his arms.

"The examination is complete, Harbart. My bride is healthy and whole. I will now take her to my personal quarters without further delay. I'm sure you can understand."

"Of course, of course. Such a disappointment, really. We shall have to inform the Prime that we missed it, right, Prince Nial?" Harbart took a small step forward, but stopped when Zane actually growled at him. Harbart held up his hands as if in surrender, but the gleam I saw in his eyes made the air catch in my throat as he continued. "Oh, commander. She is not wearing your band around her pretty little neck. Has she then, in fact, refused you already?"

The tension in the air was so thick I could barely breathe. I looked at the black strip of strange fabric in my hands and quickly lifted it to my neck. There was no clasp, but as soon as I held the ends together, they sealed, then settled against me, the collar resizing itself until it felt like a second skin.

Zane immediately relaxed and I felt the tension leave my body as well. I had pleased him, and hopefully pissed off the nasty old man who now glared at me like I'd just taken away his favorite toy.

"Ah, my mistake, commander." He bowed slightly at the waist, his long brown robe just hitting the floor in front of his boots. "My lady. Welcome to the Battleship Deston. I very much look forward to making your acquaintance again soon."

He turned on his heel and left me alone with the doctor, the prince, and my mate, who practically snarled at the prince the moment the door slid closed.

"Keep that man away from my mate, cousin, or I will kill him."

The handsome young prince wore battle armor similar to Zane's, but with slightly darker shades of browns and some black. He was big and strong, just like my mate, and his eyes were kind and very interested as he looked at me.

"Lady Deston, welcome."

When I remained silent, Zane jostled me, just enough so that I would know he expected me to speak. "Thank you." It was all I could manage. It was enough.

With a bow, the prince of Prillon Prime left us alone and

my body melted into a puddle in Zane's arms. I had no strength of will to resist or assist as Zane stood with me in his arms.

"Ah, commander. One last item for you before you take your mate to your quarters." The doctor picked up the box from the table. "Her examination did show one issue that you must resolve."

I frowned and I felt Zane tense at my back. "Oh? What issue?"

"While her pussy has been breached by another, her ass is still unclaimed. It is tight and untried."

I flushed at the doctor's words. It was true; I wasn't a virgin but no one had done *anything* to my bottom until the examination just now.

The doctor held out the dark box and then opened the lid to show us both what was inside.

My mouth fell open as I took in the array of butt plugs. I knew what they were immediately, for while I was an anal virgin, I hadn't lived under a rock. My heart, only now slowing from the earlier exam, jumped in my chest and I couldn't bear to look at them, or think about what the doctor wanted Zane to do with them.

"What... what do you need those for?" I asked.

"As part of the mating ceremony, we will claim every part of you. Your mouth, your pussy, and your ass. These—" Zane pointed at the contents of the box, "—will train you to take a cock in your bottom. It is my duty as your mate to prepare your body so you feel no pain during the claiming, only pleasure."

We? Had he said *we*?

The doctor closed the lid with a click and Zane took it from him.

"Thank you, doctor, for your concern in this matter. We will begin her training as soon as we are in my quarters."

There that word was again. We.

The doctor bowed his head.

Zane tucked the box beneath his arm and looked down

44

at me where he held me nestled against his huge chest. "Now, Hannah, I will take you to your new quarters."

I gulped once again and tried to convince my stomach that it did not need to churn and ache. Zane was going to take me back to his quarters and do… things to me. My bottom clenched just thinking about this *training*. My mind screamed at me to run, run very far away, but the collar about my neck heated and pulsed, sending a quick ripple of pleasure through my body.

I couldn't help but gasp.

The corner of Zane's mouth tipped up. "I see our collars are now linked, as they should be. From now on, you will feel my pleasure, Hannah, as I will feel yours. The link is only half strength now, temporary, but when the claiming ceremony is complete, the link will be powerful and unbreakable. It's just one of the benefits of wearing your mate's collar. Do not fear, my little human. I will bring you only pleasure, even when that virgin ass of yours is trained." When the door opened and he carried me out into the ship, all I could do was hold on as my body savored that little blissful pulse of his pleasure. He was going to do whatever he wanted to me, and trapped here, on an alien battleship in deep space, there wasn't a damn thing I could do about it.

CHAPTER FIVE

Zane

The walk to my quarters was quiet. Hannah took in the sleek green walls of the medical section of the ship, the muted blue lighting that illuminated the floor. Each section of the ship was coded with color: green for medical, red for battle, blue for engineering, and muted browns and oranges for the common areas and cafeterias. The command deck's walls were as black as deep space. It was hard to imagine this was her first glimpse of a ship in space. It wasn't just any ship, but *my* ship, and we were headed to the front.

People bowed their heads in deference as we passed, first to me, then when they saw the collar about Hannah's neck, once again, this time with their eyes wide in surprise. She noticed none of it as she took in her new surroundings. Her eyes widened as we exited the green corridors for the muted orange walls that lined the area of the ship that housed the officers' quarters.

Hannah held the sheet about her like a cape, gripping the front of it in a tight hold, clearly modest. While it was crucial she protect the sight of her naked body from others, I would teach her that there was no modesty between mates. Her body was mine and my chosen second, Dare, awaited us in

46

my quarters. Together, we would share our new mate and give her pleasure whenever and however we chose. She had much to learn and I looked forward to teaching her. I knew Dare was ready as well.

She was not born of Prillon Prime. Hannah, with her long mane of dark hair and equally dark eyes, was the antithesis of the average golden bride from my home world. She was so small, petite, and curvy! A bride of her unusual beauty would stand out and be a target under any circumstances. But she was also the bride of a commander, which would put her in even more danger. Hannah would not be able to hide among the masses. Once her claiming was complete, the color of her collar would match mine and Dare's. They were a deep blood red, as were all the collars of my family line. Should she choose, her collar could easily be hidden beneath a high-necked garment, but unless she was wrapped completely in cloth, her dramatic coloring would ensure that she would be noticed.

My knuckles turned white against the box I held. My mother had not thought this matching through. She was thinking of love and grandchildren, not the tactical aspects of war. Nor did she know of my more basic desires. Yes, Prillon warriors were known for their virility, but mine took a turn toward the extreme. I could not become too attached to this female. I could not unleash my full lust upon her, not without hurting her tiny body.

Before I'd held my small-sized mate in my arms, I had not worried about my ability to keep her safe—from me or my enemies. Nor had I concerned myself with the possibility of my own death. I had scoffed at the idea of Prillon Prime's code for mated warriors, the code of honor that demanded we name a second of our family line for our mates, another warrior to care for and protect her, to ensure her safety and well-being should the primary mate be killed.

It was only now, as my small female trembled in my arms, all soft curves and wide, innocent eyes, that I recognized the value of naming a second. As warriors, death was commonplace, especially on the front. Hannah needed protection, yet as a commander, I would be forced to be away from her often, to take risks that others would not. I would be forced to leave her side more often than I liked. I could not personally assure her safety at all times. My second, Dare, would be there for her in my absence. If something should befall me, my role as Hannah's primary mate, the father for any children we made, would fall to Dare.

The idea of her body swelling with my child made me ever more eager to rut in her pussy like a hungry animal. I would have to be careful with her, test her limits slowly. My more dominant traits would surely scare her. I wanted her to *want* me, not attempt to flee on the first transport vessel to the Prillon home world to request a new mate. Possessive instincts I'd never known rushed through me, clearing my mind and heart of all confusion.

Hannah Johnson was *mine*, and I would do anything I had to do to convince her to accept my claim, even if that meant hiding my true self. Even with Dare to protect her, I knew I *should* give her up. Mating a commander was risky business, especially me, but how could I walk away? One glimpse at her and I'd known. She *was* my mate. *She was mine.* No one else would have her but Dare. When I watched her come, when I saw her slick arousal slip out around the medical probes, when I smelled the sweet scent of it, there was no going back. I wanted her bound to my table in my secret room on level seventeen, naked, with her nipples clamped and her pussy stuffed with a vibrating dildo. There she would learn the true meaning behind the word *obey*.

I wanted to taste her, lick her, fuck her, and fill her with my seed in every tight hole while she called me *master*.

That would not happen. It couldn't happen if I were to keep her. The connection was too powerful to deny. When she slipped the collar about her neck, our bonding had begun. I felt her lingering pleasure, the pulsing hints of arousal that continued to course through her veins. She'd liked the pleasure, yet disliked how it had been wrought. That had been from a testing probe, not my mouth or my fingers or my cock. If she'd disliked a simple spanking and a medical test, then she would certainly hate being forced into true submission.

I'd disliked her exam as well, but for a completely different reason. I did not want the doctor to see her pleasure. I settled with being content knowing she was healthy, easily aroused and ripe for breeding. Mordin had confirmed she found pleasure in having her ass and pussy filled at the same time, a requirement for a Prillon bride. Just a little training and she'd be ready to take both Dare and me together. The claiming could not occur until then.

In the meantime, we could fuck her and train her. It was our duty to teach her about being claimed by two men; I knew Earth custom did not allow it. That alone was enough. Based on the way she resisted the medical examination, I was expecting her to resist Dare, to resist the idea of a second mate. That was why he had been instructed to wait in my quarters. If she could not handle my second, she would never be able to accept my true desires.

Her response to her second mate would be apparent soon enough. And when the door slid shut behind us and we were finally within the privacy of my own rooms, Dare was an unknown no longer. He stood from the long chaise placed in front of the wall of display monitors that currently showed a vista of space.

I looked around the room quickly. These were new quarters, and the ship's crew had moved mine and Dare's belongings into our new, mated quarters when Hannah arrived. There was a full lounging area with a chaise, two large reclining chairs, and a long couch. The walls were draped with soft fabrics meant to soften the austere look of the ship's hard, blank walls. Unlike in the single males' quarters, the walls were decorated with images of my home world's mountains and famous landmarks. A full-sized S-Gen unit was in the corner of the sleeping area, close to a bed that was three times larger than anything I'd slept in before.

Big enough for three. The dark red blankets were the color of our family line, and placed on the bed out of respect for the next generation that would be created there.

My gaze travelled to my second, but Dare only had eyes for Hannah. She had noticed him on our entry, but when I set her gently on her feet she did not speak to him, but moved to stand in front of the glass, seeing space, I assumed, for the first time. As she stared, the sheet slipped off her shoulders to reveal her pale skin and the long line of her neck. Dark hair curved over one shoulder and the back of the collar was visible.

Dare glanced at me and I nodded once. I heard him sigh, relieved. The collar about Hannah's neck proved she was well, but also gave us authority over her body for the next thirty days. Now that she had accepted the claiming period, she belonged to us, at least for a few weeks. It was our job to convince her to stay forever.

Perhaps it had been fortuitous that Harbart and the prince had come to the med station. While she might not have realized it, she'd placed the collar about her neck as a sign of trust in me. She knew, subconsciously through our bond, that I would keep her safe from the vile court elder.

I lifted the box for Dare to see, then placed it on the dining table. Dare's eyes widened at the sight of it just before he reached down and adjusted himself in his pants. The idea of training our mate was as arousing for him as it was for me.

"It's so beautiful," she murmured.

I'd seen the vista my entire life and saw nothing unusual about it. I could understand her awe, but she would have the rest of her life to look.

"Hannah."

When she didn't turn, I repeated, "Hannah."

Dare cleared his throat.

"I want you to meet Dare, your second mate."

As I'd anticipated, she spun on her heel and looked between me and Dare. "My second mate? I'm sorry, I'm confused." A deep V formed in her smooth brow.

Dare stepped toward her, bowed his head to show her his deepest respect, then met her gaze. "I'm Dare, Zane's named second, Hannah."

She looked up at my friend and distant cousin, the long line of her neck visible. How I wanted to kiss along that length, taste her skin there, feel the fast thrumming of her pulse. I could see the blood frantically pulsing through her veins from across the room.

"You said… second mate?"

Dare spoke before I did.

"Prillon women have two mates." Dare tilted his head in my direction. "You were matched to Zane through the bride program, but he has chosen me as his second. I have been waiting just as long to meet you. And I find you to be lovely, Hannah."

She waved off the compliment and came around Dare's large frame to stand before me. "You said I belonged to you."

"You do," I replied. "But I have chosen Dare as my second, so you belong to him as well."

She tugged at the collar about her neck, but it would not budge. "And the collars? I *felt* a connection to you. Warden Egara assured me that I was only matched to one mate. I was not matched to two of you."

"That is true. You were *matched* to me. Only me. But I choose my second and because of that, you are *mated* to both of us," I clarified as Dare came to stand beside Hannah.

He held up his new collar, currently black; it lay limp over his palm. When she turned to him, I stepped up behind her and placed my hands on her bare shoulders as Dare spoke. She was between us, just where I wanted her.

"I've been waiting for you, Hannah," he murmured. "I wanted to be with you when I put this on and made us all one."

Dare wrapped the collar about his neck as Hannah watched. The ends sealed and it turned a deep red. I felt the jolt in my body and Hannah's gasp let us both know that she felt the connection as well. With Dare joined in our bond, the connection with Hannah was stronger. I could smell the scent of her wet and eager pussy even more blatantly than before. In return, she was now feeling both of us, and our desire to pleasure her. Dare's eyes flared as he felt the first pulse of Hannah's rising arousal. I knew he could scent her, too. "I feel you now, my mate. You and I are connected, just as you are linked to Zane."

Hannah stepped back until she bumped into me. I wrapped my arm around her shoulders so that my forearm rested just below her chin. I wanted her to know that I had her, that I would always have her.

She reached up and wrapped two small, trembling hands around my forearm, but I noted that the panicked racing of her heart began to slow, and she did not push me away. She clung to me, as if I were already her true match, as if I were the only safe haven in the room. "But I can't have two mates!"

I leaned over, eager to bury my face in the silken strands of her hair, and asked my question with my lips pressed to the back of her head. "Why not?"

"It's just not done!"

Dare crossed his arms over his chest and I caught his eye to make sure we were in agreement. Yes, we would have a discussion on this topic—for a short time—then we would persuade her to accept the idea in other ways.

"On Prillon it is the only way a woman can mate," I added.

"Why?" she asked, her voice shaky.

I settled my cheek against the top of her head as Dare answered her. "Zane is commander of this ship, of an entire fleet of ships. I am a combat pilot. If something were to happen to one of us in battle, you would need a second mate to make sure you would not be left alone and unprotected.

52

We are a warrior race, Hannah. We do not expect to live long lives and we do not fear death, but we do believe in safeguarding our mates and our children. Our mating rituals were created to protect you. You will not be less than a Prillon bride simply because you are from Earth. You will be gifted with the sanctity of a double bond to ensure your future, and a future for your children."

"So, I was matched to Zane, but now I'm to just accept you as well?"

Dare grinned. "It would be easiest if you did, but I will certainly enjoy persuading you should you have doubts. Just think, Hannah. Two men to cherish you. Two men to see to your needs in and out of the bedroom."

Her hands tightened their grip on my arm as she thought of that possibility.

"Is it normal for her skin to turn that pretty shade of pink?" Dare asked me.

"Mmm, it's called blushing." I lifted my head and turned her in my arms so I could watch as the color spread from her exposed shoulders, up her neck, and into her cheeks. "Her nipples are that same shade and when she comes, her pussy flushes a slightly darker color."

Her face flushed even more at those words. "Zane!" she cried out, clearly mortified.

"There will be no secrets between us," Dare said. He touched his collar. "With the collars, there can't be. I know that the idea of being with both of us frightens your mind, but your body is excited by the idea. I can feel your pussy's ache and the heaviness of your breasts with Zane's arms rested right above them. And so can Zane." Dare licked his lips slowly, as if he couldn't wait to take a soft globe into his mouth.

Her mouth fell open and she tightened her grip on the sheet.

"I don't believe you," she whispered.

Dare undid the front of his pants and pulled out his cock. Hannah turned her head away and squeezed her eyes closed.

"You do not need to see me to know how I feel about you." Dare gripped the base of his hard cock and began stroking it, his thumb brushing over the flared head.

While my collar was programmed to mute Dare's feelings, Hannah's was programmed to fully experience the physical link with both of her mates. She would know the intensity of both our desires, both our needs when it came to her. There was no question she could feel Dare's arousal, feel the rush of pleasure just looking upon her brought to him.

She gasped and turned her head back in his direction as I rubbed her bare shoulder with my palm and whispered in her ear. "The connection, Hannah, is powerful. It can't be denied."

Dare continued to stroke and she continued to stare at him, her skin flushing impossibly darker. Her pussy was dripping wet with her arousal; I could scent it in the air. Her racing heart, her aching backside, the heavy weight of her breasts, and the throbbing demand of her pussy... all sensations came through the collar with the utmost of precision.

"I don't understand," she replied, her voice hoarse.

"You will adjust, Hannah, not only to space, but to me and Dare," I told her. "Only time will give you the knowledge you need to accept your new life. In the meantime, we will begin our life together as we mean to live it from now on. Remove the sheet."

Hannah's eyes remained on Dare's hand stroking his cock.

"Hannah," I warned. "Do as you are told."

When a bead of fluid dripped down the crown of Dare's cock, Hannah licked her lips. The subtle scent of Dare's pre-cum was an aphrodisiac, an arousal tool used to bring about desire and eagerness in our mates.

Having Dare stroke himself not only let Hannah see he had desire for her, but initiated her arousal response to him.

Once the pre-cum touched her skin, seeped into her silky flesh, the connection between them would only enhance. The sensual side effects of the pheromones in our cum would create an even deeper bond once our seed was buried deep within her.

History had proven that even if a female mate was reluctant to fuck right away, they would usually at least allow a man to show his cock and hence, be exposed to the pre-cum's sexual effects, just as Hannah was right now. She didn't know it, but her mating connection had begun. She would be eager for both of us, her pussy continually wet, her body on edge and hungry. Our desire would feed hers through the mental link forged by the collars we wore. Her mind might try to fight our lust-filled desires, but the collar and the connection we shared was strong. Dare and I were powerful warriors and even we couldn't fight it—nor did we want to.

Some cultures argued that the link was a form of coercion, a way to use a woman's own body against her. But that argument was for the unmated people on our world, for once mated, none voluntarily gave up the bond. It gave too much pleasure.

Hannah was my match. There was no need for her to fight what would ultimately bring her great happiness and safety. Neither Dare nor I wanted to waste time before claiming her. Even now the ship headed for the war at the front. We had to get past Hannah's defenses quickly and with precision. Only when we had completed the claiming ceremony and her collar matched ours would her safety be ensured.

I stepped back and dropped my hands from her shoulders to cross them over my chest. Hannah stood rooted in place, watching Dare stroke his cock. She didn't move, almost as if she wasn't sure what we expected of her. I was more than willing to remedy that.

"Turn around, Hannah, and show Dare your ass. Let him see the bright pink handprints from your punishment."

Her eyes tore from Dare's ministrations to meet mine. She could hear the implication in my words. Continue to defy me and she would be spanked again.

She didn't move and I took one small step closer, but kept my voice smooth and gentle. I was not angry with her, and I needed to be sure she knew that.

"Take off the sheet."

As she swallowed, she released her tight hold on the covering and it fell to the floor.

Dare groaned at the sight of her. Dark hair fell over her shoulder to brush against one pink nipple. Her breasts were full, more than a handful, with large, plump tips. As we watched, they hardened into tight peaks. She wasn't slim like Prillon women, but soft and round. Her waist was slightly curved and her hips were wide and a perfect, lush hold for our hands as we fucked her.

Lower, between her thighs, the slick folds of her pussy were visible. They glistened, pink and swollen, from her earlier pleasure. She grew aroused as the link between us flared. I knew she was feeling my need to lick her pussy and hear her sweet cries as she came all over my mouth. The painful fullness of my cock would reach her senses as well. I was as hard as Dare, eager to sink inside her supple body. The scent of her arousal grew stronger now, sweet and potent.

Dare inhaled deeply and I knew he'd noticed it as well.

"Very good, Hannah. I am proud of you for showing us your body. What is yours, is ours," Dare commented. "Our breasts, our nipples, our pussy, our ass. Even those reddened bottom cheeks."

"She needed some early guidance," I clarified.

While she squirmed uncomfortably beneath our gazes, she kept her hands at her sides.

"Doctor Mordin found her in perfect health, although there was one deficiency. Her ass is tight, too tight for a proper claiming."

Hannah shook her head as she looked at Dare's cock

again. "That… it won't fit. Of course I'm tight, if that's what the doctor used as a guide."

I grinned and I saw Dare smile as well. "Ah, Hannah, I enjoy the flattery, as does Dare, but we are already your mates. It is unnecessary."

She flicked her gaze to me. "I didn't mean it as flattery," she countered. "He's… he's huge!"

I began to undo my pants as I spoke. I could feel the pre-cum leaking from my swollen tip. She needed to be exposed to the subtle scent of it for what we planned next. I could spank her, but training her ass would be more successful, much more rewarding for all of us, if she were eager for it.

"Dare's cock is big." I parted the flaps and pulled myself free. "But so is mine."

Hannah's mouth fell open as she stared at my cock. I'd read that Prillon men were much larger than those on Earth, in all parts of their anatomy. We were often a head taller, more muscular and broader, genetically ready for battle. Our cocks, too, were an impressive size, crucial to pleasing our mates, filling them completely to ensure the most perfect bond, the most intense pleasure for our women so that our seed would take root.

Pre-cum dribbled from the tip and I swiped it with my thumb. I closed the distance to Hannah and placed the wet fluid on her bottom lip. She gasped in surprise, for I'd moved swiftly. As I slid my thumb back and forth across that plump flesh, her eyes widened. They were so dark that I almost didn't see the centers narrow to fine points. Instinctively, her tongue flicked out and took the moisture into her mouth. I watched as her vision blurred.

"The fluid from our cocks will mix with your own arousal. Your body will soften, open and be ready for us. When we fuck you, I promise it will not hurt. You will beg us to take you, mate, and you will scream your pleasure."

I felt the soft fan of her breath on my hand in quick short bursts as she tried to control her reaction. Watching the effects of my body's mating fluid working on her was heady.

"Zane, the doctor said she needs her ass trained?" Dare asked, his voice deeper than I'd ever heard it. He, too, was affected.

I moved back to the table to retrieve the box of plugs. Dare took Hannah's hand and led her to the chaise. He sat and pulled her to stand directly before him. In this position, her breasts were in front of his hungry mouth and Dare obviously couldn't resist the temptation, for his long tongue snaked out and circled one nipple, sampling it, then pulling and tugging on it.

Hannah's knees bent and she gripped Dare's shoulders for support. A sigh escaped her lips before she shook her head, trying to fight the sensual fog I knew clouded her mind, as her desire clouded mine. "No, this isn't right. I don't even know you, Dare."

Dare sat back and looked up at her. "As Zane's second, we are mated, connected." He tugged at his collar. "Do not fight what is right."

They stared into each other's eyes and the collar let me know that Hannah wanted Dare to suck on her plump breasts. She wanted his tongue on her skin.

"Up on the chaise, Hannah. Get on your hands and knees," I said. If she were to argue like this about simply showing us her body and getting ready for us to fuck her, then she definitely couldn't handle my more aggressive needs.

"No. I can't. This isn't right. I shouldn't want this. Not two of you. I can't do this."

Dare lifted her and easily moved her into the position I wanted, with her grumbling the entire time. Once in place, Dare came to stand beside me as we both enjoyed the view of her upturned, heart-shaped ass.

"Yes, I see you had a time of it in the medical center."

I actually chuckled, but Hannah began to move.

"Comm Unit, restraints," I said loudly. The room's computer system responded and the hidden bindings came out of the chaise.

Dare moved to encircle one of her wrists to the restraint that was set low on one leg of the chair, then the other. I wrapped a long strap over the back of her calves, securing them into her current position.

"Hey! I don't like this!" Hannah cried out, struggling against the bonds. Her breasts and head were pressed against the soft cushion of the chaise with her ass up in the air. She could wiggle her hips, but could not move otherwise.

She was in the perfect position to be fucked, but also to have her ass trained. One would happen now, the other later. Definitely later.

Besides her reddened ass, her pussy was open and on display. Bare, as required for all female mates, her slick folds glistened in the soft lights recessed in the ceiling. As she squirmed, the swollen petals parted.

Dare hissed at the sight of the tight entrance to her sheath, her arousal dripping from it and down her creamy thighs. Her clit was exposed, thrusting proudly outward from the little hood, eager for our touch. Her body was so responsive, so in tune to the connection we shared.

"She's ready for us," Dare growled. "But even with the spanking, she obviously has not yet learned to obey her mates." He lifted his hand to gently caress Hannah's still pink bottom.

Hannah pressed her head against the chaise. "I'm not a robot. I don't obey orders like one. I just met you both. I… I can't have two husbands. Please…"

We both heard the plaintive tone to her voice. Our pretty little mate was confused and scared. But disobedience on a battleship was never tolerated, from warriors under my command or from my mate. Evidently, Dare agreed.

I watched as Dare explored her wet folds with his fingers. He ran his hand along her back and hips, petting her until she calmed enough to listen to reason. Then he made our expectations clear. "You will obey us, Hannah. Without

GRACE GOODWIN

question. Or you will be punished." He leaned over and placed a gentle kiss at the small of her back. "I am going to spank you now, Hannah. And the next time we tell you to ready your body for us, you will do so without argument."

"What? No!"

Her protests were cut off by the sharp crack of Dare's hand striking her ass. "Count to ten, Hannah."

Dare intentionally struck her bottom where she was still pink from her earlier discipline. She cried out the count, her breasts swaying beneath her as Dare's swats rocked her body back and forth on her knees.

I stood, taking it all in, growing harder with the resounding clap of each smack on her round ass. Her cries of protest turned to sobs, and finally moans as her body's natural responses kicked in, flooding her system with liquid fire. Her pussy was wetter than it had been before Dare began spanking her, the bright red marks on her naked bottom a woman's most primitive call to her mate.

When Dare finished, he leaned over her, whispering in her ear. "We will fuck you now, Hannah, in your mouth and in that wet little pussy."

From my vantage point behind her I saw her pussy clench with lust at his words. She wanted us. She wanted this.

Evidently, our bride's mind was at war with her body. "This was a mistake. You're just going to use me."

"We will *never* use you, Hannah." Moving to kneel beside her, I stroked her sleek hair back from her face. "We'll fuck you, but always give you your pleasure. Always."

"But for now, we need to stretch that tight ass of yours, to get you ready for our cocks."

She tried to shake her head. "I've never… I don't want that."

"That's right, you've never had anything in that virgin ass of yours until earlier today. You won't know if you don't want it or not until you've tried it," I added.

"We're going to take such good care of you, Hannah,"

Dare said, opening the box and taking out a bottle of the lubrication fluid. "The claiming ceremony will have me in your ass and Zane in your pussy. Only then will your collar change to match ours as we become one."

I settled behind her and cupped her pussy in the palm of my hand. It was hot and wet and so very soft. Gently, I stroked her there, learning the feel of her, the way she liked to have her clit stroked. I explored her pussy, learned how to stroke and tease inside her wet core, learning what made her jump and cry out and whimper with need.

It didn't take long for Hannah's eyes to fall shut and for her to succumb to my touch. I wasn't sure how I would survive the feel of her. My cock ached with a desperate need to fuck her, but this wasn't about my needs, but hers.

Dare opened the bottle and put a small drop of the slick fluid onto his two fingers, then brushed them over the tight rosette of her ass.

"Oh, God!" she cried as Dare circled the lubrication against her tender skin.

"Shh, Hannah, let us make you feel good. That's it. Relax all your muscles. You aren't in charge. Your body belongs to us. Give over and we'll make you come again and again."

We continued touching her, slowly and patiently as if we had no reason to rush. We didn't. We'd been waiting our whole lives for Hannah. I may not have wanted to find her—but now that she was here, there was no question she was mine. She was Dare's.

Moving the bottle close to her tight entrance, Dare told her what he was going to do. "Relax, that's the narrow tip of a bottle of lubrication fluid. It's small, smaller than the probe the doctor used. That's it, push out and let it in."

"Good girl," I added, curling my fingers to rub over the sensitive spot inside her pussy.

She cried out and clenched her hands into fists. Her skin was slick with sweat and the scent of her was hot and ripe. I was glad my cock was free from the confines of my pants, for it would have been painful otherwise. My own eagerness flowed from the opening. The way she responded to us, I had no doubt our own scents were arousing her as hers affected us.

"You're going to feel the fluid filling you. Yes, it's nice and warm."

She shifted her hips as Dare squeezed the bottle.

"That's going to make you nice and slick inside, hot and wet. Once you're properly stretched for us, we're going to slide in so nice and easy. You're going to love it. There, that's all of it. You did so well, Hannah."

Dare dropped the empty bottle on the chaise and found the smallest plug. He held it up for me and I shook my head. He traded it for the next size up. It was the size of my thumb, but longer. It would stretch her some, but fill her deep. Her body needed to accommodate not only to the width of our cocks, but the long length as well.

With my two fingers inside her pussy, I stroked my thumb over the left side of her clit, very lightly as it was exposed from its protective hood.

She gasped as I did so, but the sound turned to a groan as Dare pressed the plug against her untried hole.

"That's the plug. That's right, it's nice and slick. Push back. Again. I know you can take it, Hannah."

She was panting now, her face scrunched up as she fought against Dare's entry. I should spank her for disobedience, but that would only make her clench down. Instead, I pressed more firmly against her clit and slid my fingers in deeper, working her now, building her toward her first mate-given orgasm.

Her body softened immediately as she cried out at my more aggressive attentions to her clit. Dare took that moment to carefully work the plug into her. I watched as the ring of muscle stretched and stretched, until the broadest part of the plug breached her. Once it began to taper again, Dare was able to slide the remainder of the plug's length in until it settled inside her. A small base kept it in place.

"Dare, I… it's so big. I can't…" She closed her eyes with a soft, keening sound before pressing her wet pussy harder into my hand as I increased the pace of my strokes. "Yes, Zane! More!"

I grinned at her varying emotions, unsure one minute if she liked a plug in her ass, the next loving the feel of my thumb on her clit.

A perk of two mates was four hands upon her. Mine were occupied with her pussy and clit. Dare tugged at the base of the plug, awakening all the little nerve endings that would bring Hannah intense pleasure when we fucked her ass. His other hand stroked over her sore bottom, awakening all the heated skin from her earlier spanking.

"Such a good girl, Hannah. Come for us. Come for your mates."

She came on command, the walls of her pussy clenching down on my two fingers as if trying to draw them in deeper. She cried out and tossed her head, her long hair whipping down her back and over her ass, covering Dare's large hand where it rested on her pink cheek.

"Gorgeous," Dare murmured.

When only little ripples of her pussy squeezed my fingers, I slipped them free and licked them. The sweet taste of her coated my tongue.

I'd held out long enough. "It's time to fuck you now, Hannah."

CHAPTER SIX

Hannah

I should have been a puddle of melted female on the chaise after their attentions and the mind-blowing orgasm. Instead, Zane's words made my entire body quiver in anticipation. The scent of their bodies, and the taste of Zane's pre-cum made my lower lip tingle. Not only did I feel the training device in my ass, but the honest and nearly uncontrollable desire of my two mates. The collar around my neck buzzed without a moment's rest, sending waves of want, of need, through my entire being.

It was heady, and I felt like the most powerful, most desired woman in existence to bring not just one giant warrior, but two to the very brink of their control. Their need made me feel beautiful and feminine and hungry to please them. My rational mind tried to tell me that all these emotions, theirs and mine, couldn't be real, that these two alien males couldn't possibly care about me, long for me, and desire me with a passion bordering on pain.

But I told that little voice in my head to shut the hell up. I was bent on my hands and knees, bound, restrained, and naked halfway across the galaxy with two huge alien cocks in plain view, both eager to claim my body as their own.

Logical or not, there wasn't a damn thing I could do about it. Not now. I belonged to these two men; it was the way of their world, their custom.

Zane tugged at the restraint over my calves and released it as Dare did the same to my hands. He helped me up so that I was settled on my hands and knees.

"I doubt you need restraints now, do you, Hannah?" Zane asked.

I shook my head. No, I didn't need to be bound. I *needed* to be fucked.

As he moved to stand behind me, his huge hands wrapped around my hips, pulling my body toward him until my knees were on the edge of the chaise and my feet dangled in empty air on either side of his knees.

"Are you ready, Hannah? Are you ready for your mate?"

Zane rubbed the head of his cock over my pussy lips and I felt the scalding flare of his pre-cum as it spread over my body, blending with my own wet juices. The heat of it spread almost instantly as my hungry body absorbed his essence. I moaned and pressed back, trying to take him inside my body, at least a little. I was afraid it was going to hurt. He was huge, and my ass was still stretched by the plug Dare had inserted, but I was beyond caring.

I wanted it to hurt a little. I wanted to feel stretched and so full I couldn't take any more. I wanted to please him. I wanted to make him lose control. I wanted to be whatever he needed me to be. He positioned his huge cock at my entrance and pushed inside me slowly, barely breaching me. Just a tease. A taste of him. I squirmed and tried to push back, to take more of him, but the hands on my hips prevented my movement, which just made me want to move all the more.

"Yes. Please. Do it. Do it now."

Dare chuckled where he stood on my left side, reaching beneath me to tug on a dangling breast. He rolled my nipple between his fingers hard, before softly kneading the entire breast in his hand. I moaned and Zane growled behind me.

"She likes it, Dare. Her pussy is so wet I could take her with one thrust."

The idea made my pussy clench around his cock, trying to draw him deeper. With a growl, Zane took the tender lobes of my spanked bottom and gripped them none too gently with his two strong hands. He pulled them apart hard, until the pain of my sore bottom raced through my bloodstream like liquid fire and my pussy lips were pulled impossibly wide.

"So beautiful, Hannah." I knew Zane was staring at my pussy, at the pink folds stretched around the head of his cock. How he had such control, such patience, I didn't know, but I didn't want to wait. I was so frustrated, I was near the point of tears.

"Please. I can't wait. I need…"

Zane pushed forward, spreading me a bit more, then stopped.

I cried out as I dropped my head, and the sound was very close to a sob.

That sound, my complete surrender, broke him. I felt his body sing with anticipation through our connection less than a second before Zane slammed deep in one powerful thrust.

He moved behind me like a piston, his cock angled to stroke the sweet spot inside me and his huge hands holding my ass cheeks spread wide so he could bottom out inside me, impossibly hard and deep.

Beside me, Dare's touch drifted like a flame following a trail of gasoline from my nipple to my clit as he knelt on the floor beside me. He angled his head to claim my nipple with his mouth, his long tongue tugging and tasting as his hand stroked my clit while Zane fucked me. The erotic image of the two strong warriors working my body was the final push I needed to lose myself. These men were mine now. Mine.

I said the word aloud as the orgasm rolled over me, pulling me under like an undertow at the beach and I screamed, for the first time in my life, completely out of control.

Dare waited until the throes of my pleasure had lessened, then shifted position to straddle the seat in front of me. His legs hung off either side, and his cock was before me, mere inches from my mouth.

I knew what he wanted. I could feel the nearly desperate need riding him. I could scent the pre-cum that seeped from the tip. I licked my lips, salivating to taste it.

As Zane's cock slowed its pace in my pussy, I leaned over and licked the pre-cum from the crown of Dare's huge cock. I felt like a sexual goddess, naughty and filled with feminine power as his essence melted into my tongue, pushing me right back to the brink of another orgasm.

Holy shit. What was in these alien warriors' cum that turned me into a raging nymphomaniac?

Zane slammed into my pussy hard, which nudged the plug into me deeply, and I decided I didn't want to know. I didn't care.

I opened my mouth wide and took as much of Dare as I could, swallowing him until his cock hit the back of my throat. I worked him with my tongue for as long as I could, enjoying his quiet growl.

Dare's pleasure drove Zane to make sure I noticed him behind me, and he released his hold on my ass to bury his hand in my hair, gripping me by the back of the neck. He held me in place over Dare's cock as his other hand slid around my hip to stroke my clit. With his hand in my hair, he guided my pace, pulling me back to torment Dare every time I tried to take him deep again. Zane was in control here, of my pleasure and Dare's, and he wanted us both to know it.

"Suck his cock, Hannah. Suck him until his cum is running down your throat. It will trigger your next orgasm."

The guttural command, combined with the sting of his grip on my hair, set something wild loose inside me. Something foreign and powerful. And this primitive side of me reveled in their domination, craved their pleasure more than my own, needed to please them both. Dare's satisfaction hummed through my collar, making me feel like a conquering queen, like the most powerful woman in the galaxy, the sexiest, hottest female alive. But Zane? Zane's emotions were a web of lust and darkness, of desire and restraint.

Zane was holding himself back. He was in firm control, riding me, feeling my tight, hot pussy but wanting more, needing something more than I was giving him.

Deep within me, the need to please him, to make him happy roared to life inside me. In that moment, I was not complete unless he was pleased with me, unless I'd satisfied that darkness in him, unless I'd brought him peace. I wanted a happy mate. If these men were mine, if this was to be my life, I *needed* them to be pleased. My own pleasure dimmed as I realized Zane was not riding the edge as Dare and I were. Zane was here, but he was also hiding himself, holding back.

I whimpered, determined to satisfy my primary mate, my match. I was supposed to be perfect for him, and he was supposed to be perfect for me. If I couldn't satisfy him, there must be something wrong with me. Perhaps there was no man in the entire universe who I could truly love.

The thought made me sad, and desperate to pull Zane out of his darkness.

I sucked Dare's cock deeper than I'd ever taken any man, swallowing around him until his cock was partially down my throat. His growl encouraged me as I rose and fell over him.

Dare came, his cock bucking and writhing in my mouth like a living beast, a beast I'd tamed, a beast that was mine to command, mine to pleasure. Dare's pleasure flooded me and my heart melted toward this strange warrior. He was very pleased, his contentment coursing through me and making me happy.

But Zane? He let go of my hair and wildly thrust into me, one hand on my clit and one dangerously close to the plug filling my ass. Yes, I wanted this. I wanted Zane to be a little wild.

Then he moved the plug, just enough to make me feel like I was being taken by both of my mates at once, fucked in both places and fingered.

The searing cum sliding down my throat set off my own release, just as Zane had said. My screams were muffled by the thick cock stretching my mouth wide. Feeling both Dare's orgasm and Zane's imminent release through my collar only accentuated my own pleasure until I was almost delirious. Overcome.

I released Dare's cock, afraid I would bite as my pleasure crested. Zane's cock moved of its own volition deep inside me, his hips slapping against my sore ass. His release, the hot splash of his seed inside me, triggered another of my own and I went rigid and silent, unable to draw enough air to scream. I had none left.

I came back to myself slowly, as if I were in a daze. And indeed, that's what I felt like. This wild, wanton sexual creature couldn't be me.

Zane's hand moved up and down my sweaty back with long, slow strokes with his cock still buried deep inside me. His body was sated, but I could sense his frustration, his need to do more, his need for me to be more.

Dare rose and placed soft kisses on every part of my skin he came near, completely at peace. Happy. Sated.

But not Zane. Zane had fucked me and I could sense he was hiding his disappointment behind a soft smile and softer touch. I wanted to cry, but I bit my lip and hid my face from both of my mates.

I had not pleased him. He was dissatisfied in me, and that knowledge made my heart hurt. I barely knew these men, but they were mine and I was theirs. I needed Zane to be pleased with me. I needed it with a desperation I'd never felt before.

But I'd given them everything. I had nothing else to offer him. Nothing.

The urgency was gone from all three of us, leaving a

languid contentment in my body. I'd never been so well used, so completely and totally owned, body and soul. Part of me relished the feeling, but part of me could just hear my mother's disapproving voice telling me that everything that had just happened in this room was wrong. Two men? A butt plug? Taking one cock in my mouth and one in my pussy, and loving it?

Wrong. Wrong. Wrong. I'd been seduced to the dark side. I'd turned into a slut, a whore, a dozen different slurs raced through my mind. I was a good girl, wasn't I? Maybe not. Maybe I was bad. Maybe I was corrupted. Maybe Zane wanted me to resist them? Maybe he wanted me to fight them? Or reject Dare? Maybe, deep down, he didn't want me to enjoy both of them?

I had no way of knowing, and I couldn't ask him in front of Dare. Hell, I wasn't sure I had the courage to ask him anything at all. He was the commander of an entire fleet of ships. Maybe he just wasn't made to be happy. Maybe, even after what he'd said, he didn't really want a mate at all.

As Dare continued to stroke my skin, Zane gently pulled his cock free. Suddenly on my own, I collapsed onto the chaise and curled into a ball around myself. I didn't know what to do. I didn't know what to think or say or feel. I felt lost. Just a few hours in outer space and I'd turned into a woman I didn't recognize. I'd let two men I didn't know fuck me and use my body in ways I'd never imagined. And I'd liked it. I'd come all over Zane's cock like I couldn't wait for more. And it wasn't enough for him. The collar's link between me and my men, while so arousing during sex, was now a curse. Without it, I wouldn't know of Zane's disappointment. I wouldn't feel like I'd failed him somehow.

Just as I was working myself up into a state, Zane's strong arms wrapped around me. He lifted me and settled me across his lap, my ear above his beating heart and my body curled up in his arms like a small child's. He was huge, a monster among men. My monster.

"What troubles you, Hannah?" One hand stroked my back and the other he lifted to settle against the side of my face and neck, holding me to him as Dare sat beside us and ran his hands over my hair.

I couldn't speak. There was no way to explain the chaotic swirl of emotions that threatened to explode out of me in a crying fit that would put a two-year-old's temper tantrum to shame.

To my relief, they didn't push me for answers, just held me and petted me as if I were the most precious thing in the universe.

After several long minutes I got myself back under control and relaxed in Zane's arms. I even managed a smile at Dare, who watched me with concerned green eyes, very unlike Zane's. Now that I had time to process and think, I noticed he was slightly darker, his coloring more dramatic, and his eyes were a deep green, like summer grass, not dark amber like Zane's.

Dare was gorgeous, too, but in his own way. He was several inches shorter than Zane, and his shoulders weren't quite as broad, but were still massive.

I looked my fill, studying the hard angles of his face, and realizing that he was still clothed. They were both still fully clothed, only their cocks were free. Their still hard cocks. For some reason, that irritated the hell out of me.

"Why am I the only one naked?"

Dare's smile was infectious. "Because you're the most beautiful."

I grinned. Flattery was going to get him nowhere. "I disagree." They were both beautiful, my mates. But I didn't know anything about them. "Who are you, Dare? You said you're a pilot, but what do you do?"

He rubbed a strand of my long black hair between his fingers as if the color fascinated him. "I am a pilot, Hannah. I am the leader of the ninth battle wing."

"Another soldier." I leaned against Zane, grateful when he seemed to know what I needed without me having to ask. He wrapped both arms around me and held me tight, so I wouldn't float away in a sea of panic. Their explanation for the need all Prillon warriors had to name a second suddenly felt a lot more real. I barely knew these two strong men, but I didn't want them to die. The thought made me shiver as pain lanced behind my eyes. "What does that mean? What is a battle wing?"

"I feel your worry, mate. Do not fear. We fly the small fighters, designed for scouting missions, tight places and direct, ship-to-ship combat."

I imagined a scene from my favorite movie in which the small ships zipped around each other in space firing lasers and blowing each other to smithereens at lightning speed. My heart, which had barely recovered from our sexual play, began to thunder in my chest as I imagined Dare in one of those ships, being chased. Fired at. Blown up.

God, what had I done? What was I supposed to do here on this battleship? Accept these two warriors, wait a few weeks or months for one of them to die, and just get a new mate every time? I knew myself too well for that. My heart wouldn't be able to take it.

It wasn't just this fear of their deaths that worried me. That was more than enough, but I sensed something through the collar. There was no explanation for it, but I knew I was attuned to these men in ways I never imagined. There was this feeling, this nudging concern that Zane knew more than he was saying, as if he were keeping a secret, hiding something from me.

Did he know something about their imminent deaths he wasn't telling me? As commander of the ship, of a fleet of ships, surely he would know the status of this war I'd transported into. What wasn't he telling me and why did I feel that without this secret, I could never accept his claim?

Was this why he held back during our sexual play? Was this secret the darkness I felt in him? Had he brought me halfway across the universe knowing he was going to die? Or was he concealing something else? Another lover? A woman he wanted more than me? A past he feared I couldn't accept? Did he find me lacking in some fundamental way?

I shoved at Zane's arms, feeling like I'd just given my body to a complete stranger. I had given these men my body, gave over, *submitted* to them both. I let them shove a plug up my ass and their cocks in my pussy and mouth. I'd given in to the pleasure they knew how to wring from my body. Yet they wouldn't give everything in return. Zane was holding back and surely Dare knew, surely he could feel it, too.

Zane let me go and I stood on shaky legs, feeling like a newborn kitten. I couldn't live like this. Not forever. The matching program must have made a mistake. I couldn't trust Zane with my heart if he was keeping secrets. "I think—I need to go home now."

CHAPTER SEVEN

Hannah

Both warriors jumped to their feet at my words.

"No," Zane barked at me.

"Why, Hannah? What have we done to upset you?"

I shook my head and wandered the edges of the room, looking for anything I could wear. The sheet that I'd dropped to the floor wouldn't do for interplanetary travel. I needed to find one of those transporter things and tell them to send me home. I couldn't deal with their way of life, their secrets. Bad enough that I was expected to fall in love with a warrior who could die at any moment. Zane, my match, was so sure of his impending death, in fact, he chose a second man to take care of me when it inevitably happened? And in the meantime, he kept things from me? My match. I was supposed to give him everything. Surrender myself, body and soul. Yet he was allowed to remain a mystery, to hide the deepest part of himself? What if I accepted his claim, tied myself to him for life, and then found out he was actually freaking crazy? Or insanely jealous? Or abusive.

No. I couldn't accept Zane with his true self in shadows. I'd made that mistake before, on Earth, and knew it to be insanity. I'd just have to survive long enough to get out of this mess without falling in love with either one of them. "This is a mistake. I'm sorry. I just—I can't do this. I have to go home."

Dare looked at Zane, clearly at a loss, and shrugged. Zane tucked his cock back into his pants and frowned. "Hannah, you *are* home."

"No." I glanced around at the strangely colored brownish walls, the window where, even now, stars and galaxies raced by in a never-ending stream of what looked like shooting stars. The furniture was bolted to the floors and the art on the walls depicted landscapes that felt all wrong, with skies that weren't blue, and two or three moons hanging above the landscape. I wanted a blue sky, and trees, and soft green grass under my bare feet. I wanted chocolate and coffee and a man to love who wasn't going to go off and do his best to get himself killed tomorrow or the next day, or next week. "I have to go home, back to Earth."

Zane looked over his shoulder at Dare. "Go prepare a bath for our mate."

Dare nodded and left me alone with my matched mate, the one perfect man for me in all the universe. The warrior I was destined to lose.

I turned on my heel and picked up the sheet, but before I could put it around my body, Zane's arms wrapped around me from behind and I was suddenly held with my back to his chest. His muscular arms surrounded me, one at my waist and one at my shoulders. I couldn't move, and for some bizarre reason I couldn't explain, even to myself, that calmed me enough to think. Being confined and held securely soothed me.

"Hannah, tell me what's bothering you. Were we too rough with you? Did we take you too hard?"

I could feel the heat rushing to my face at his question. The answer was no. Not too hard. Not too fast. I'd loved it. It hadn't been as aggressive as the processing dream, the recorded claiming I'd witnessed, but it had been… amazing.

"No, Zane. You didn't hurt me." In fact, I wanted more.

I wanted my warriors to dominate my body and make me come over and over. I wanted to give them everything—but I was afraid. That annoying weakness I had for dominant, alpha males was rearing its ugly head. And Zane was truly my match. I could feel the connection between us—and Dare as well—as easily as I could feel his touch on my skin. It was real and solid and so strong already that it felt like a tangible thing between us. I wanted to know everything about my men. I wanted to truly belong to them. I wanted to claim them as mine forever and trust in the matching program, or God, or whatever bizarre twist of fate had brought me to this place, to this warrior. I wanted to fall head over heels in love with both of them and hold nothing back. Nothing. And *that* was the problem. I would give them everything, heart, mind and soul, and it wasn't going to be enough. Zane's darkness spread, his discontent coming through my collar as clearly as a bell ringing inside my head. I wasn't enough for him. I wasn't enough, and he just couldn't bring himself to tell me.

"Hannah, talk to me, or I will have you over my knee."

I squirmed at his threat, my bottom still sore from its earlier spanking and the plug still filling me. I knew he wasn't making idle threats. I sighed, and decided I might as well tell him the truth, or at least as much of it as I could. His darkness and the hurt it caused me? I had some pride. That I would keep to myself. "I can't be your mate, Zane. I'm sorry. I know the computer or whatever matched us, but I can't do this."

"You fear our deaths. I can sense your sadness, Hannah, your fear. We're all going to die, Hannah. Death is part of life. Is it our death you fear, or is it me? Do you wish to test another? Are you invoking your right to claim a new mate?" His voice was soft, deathly quiet, and I heard Dare's quiet footsteps as he approached from behind, listening to our conversation.

"No. I don't want another warrior." His grip loosened slightly and I took a deep breath. "I don't want to be a bride.

I want to go home." I spoke from the heart, and I knew he'd hear the sincerity of my words. I couldn't allow myself to fall in love with him. It would be a complete disaster. The idea of a perfect love, of an intense, all-consuming love, was exciting and fun and something every woman on Earth dreamed about. The reality of knowing I'd lose one of them, or both, was too intense, too much for me, especially when I knew Zane was hiding from me, that he wasn't going to love me in return. I was scared. A chicken. I admitted it, didn't try to deny it.

The silence grew heavy and thick in the air as I waited for his response. If I gave them everything, and one of them died, I wouldn't survive it. I'd crumble into a million tiny pieces of dust and drift away on the wind. Faced with the very real possibility of having the kind of man I'd always wanted, the kind I could completely lose myself in, I was terrified. They would own me. Body and soul. I would belong to them, but Zane? I could sense the shadow in him, and it was growing stronger. He would hide forever. I could feel his determination through our link. And he was the commander, the most disciplined warrior in the entire interstellar fleet. If he decided to hold himself apart, there wasn't a damn thing I could do about it. He would never truly belong to me. I couldn't live with that.

Two beeps filled the air. "Commander."

Zane stiffened behind me. "Yes," he said to the room at large.

"You are needed on the command deck." The room had some kind of ship-wide communication system.

"On my way. Deston out."

Dare cleared his throat. "Her bath is ready."

Zane sighed. "We'll discuss this later, Hannah." His arms tightened for a brief moment before he turned with me in his arms and handed me off to Dare.

Dare nodded and Zane left the room without another word. I knew I'd hurt him somehow, wounded the most formidable commander in the Prillon fleet. But he'd asked for the truth. The truth that I was petrified to be permanently tied to him and then have him die on me, or live, but never be mine. Either possibility brought me nothing but heartbreak.

"Come, Hannah. There is nowhere for you to go. Let's set your fears aside for now. Let me help you in the bath." Dare held out his hand and I took it, allowing him to lead me through the small door I'd glimpsed off to the side of the main room. He was right. Where was I to go? I had no clothes, no way to get home. I could tell Dare was trying to soothe me; I was overwhelmed. The conversation wasn't over. My concerns hadn't been resolved, but I would wait. A bath did sound good. I was sticky and sore.

It was odd to walk with the plug deep inside me. "Dare," I said, looking anywhere but at him. "What about… um, well…"

Perhaps he had an idea as to my problem or perhaps he could sense it through the collars.

"The plug stays in. It is a training plug, not a pleasure plug."

I frowned, for I didn't know the difference between the two, but I could tell by the look on his face that he would not be swayed. I sighed and took in the bathroom. It wasn't huge, but it was luxurious, with glowing white fixtures that looked like they were made of fire opals lit from within. A full tub of water awaited me. The bath was huge, large enough to easily fit two, if not all three of us. Dare tugged the sheet from my body and stripped off his uniform to reveal a chest lined with muscles, a broad strong back that tapered to thin hips and powerful legs. His cock hung, still semi-hard between his legs, the sight reminding me of his taste, of the flavor of his cum as it spilled down my throat.

"Stop looking at me like that, Hannah, or I'll fuck that sweet mouth again." In one fast motion, he lifted me off my feet and stepped into the warm water, immersing us both up to our shoulders in the scented bath.

Pressed to his naked chest, I could smell him, his scent

rising from his skin to soothe me. I'd known him such a short time, but already my body recognized his. I knew the taste of his cock and the scent of his flesh. I craved the taste of his cum, like a drug addict on Earth and the next fix. I was losing it. That was the only explanation.

Dare settled me in front of him in the bath and bathed my entire body with a strange soap that smelled like some exotic fruit as soon as it made contact with my skin. On his hand, it smelled like him, a dark, musky fragrance that made me want to press my face to his chest and just breathe him in and out of my body.

"Lean back, Hannah. I want to wash your hair." His voice seemed to invade my senses and give me a sense of comfort and safety.

I felt like a child in the swimming pool as he pulled my head back with his hands and pushed my bottom away from him so that I floated on my back in the water. He held me gently as he soaked my hair, then sat me up to massage my scalp. It felt so good I let myself go limp in his arms. I was tired and overwhelmed, and his gentle touch soothed something inside me that I hadn't realized needing soothing.

I was still trying to wrestle with the idea of two mates, but the idea was not as out of bounds as I'd once thought. Not if my mates were Zane and Dare. However, it wasn't loving them that scared the hell out of me. No, I was afraid of losing them. But even if I could force myself to face that fear, I had another fear, a darker, much more frightening one—not being loved back, not being enough for my matched mate. It wouldn't be the first time a man found me lacking.

Dare finished with me and lifted me from the tub to wrap me in a plush gray towel. He dried himself, then tended to my hair with another, squeezing the wet ends until I stopped dripping on the floor.

"Come, Hannah." He looked like a sexual god with his towel hung low over his waist and I couldn't stop staring as I placed my small hand in his much larger one. "Are you hungry? We'll get dressed and I'll take you to the dining hall."

"I don't have any clothes." I'd worn nothing but a sheet since my arrival. How was I supposed to go out in public like this?

"Trust me."

I followed him back into the main living quarters and he led me to a small black platform in the far corner. The base was covered with a grid made of green lines. Dare walked to me and leaned down to give me a soft, sweet kiss.

"Take off the towel and stand in the center. The ship will measure you and create whatever you need."

His soft voice and gentle kiss settled me and I felt like a contented kitten as I allowed him to remove my towel. I stepped naked onto the platform and held still as an array of soft green lights scanned every inch of my body. My collar tingled and buzzed and I froze at the strange sensation. When the lights disappeared, Dare held out his hand and I stepped down with my fingers on my collar. "What was that? It buzzed."

"That was the collar communicating directly with the ship's systems. Your identification and measurements have been updated in the ship's S-Gen."

"S-Gen?" So much weird stuff to learn. I truly felt out of my depth as the now empty platform lit up with bright green light that was concentrated at the base. I couldn't tear my eyes from the spectacle and when the lights were gone, a lump of fabric lay on the platform.

"Spontaneous matter generator." Dare bent over and picked up the fabric. When he lifted it for me, I saw that it was a knee-length tunic of some sort with strange leggings connected beneath it. Dare handed it to me and I discovered that it was open in the back. I stepped into the leggings and pulled it up, shoving my arms into the long sleeves. As soon as I had it on, the material closed itself in the back, fitting me like a second skin. Dare looked me over, his gaze lingering on the slightly scooped neckline that prominently displayed my collar. His attention drifted down to my breasts and waist, to the slightly flared skirt that fell almost to my knees. Beneath that, the leggings covered me completely to my ankles and my bare feet looked oddly out of place.

Dare pressed his hand to an indentation on the side of the S-Gen. "Boots for Lady Deston." At his command, the green light returned, leaving a pair of matching boots that would cover me to just above the ankle. He held them out and I slid my feet into them. I thought they would feel odd without socks, but the boots contracted around my feet just like the clothing had around my body and they were soft as silk on the inside.

Deston ordered clothing for himself as well and put on a fresh uniform and boots before taking both of our towels and my sheet and rolling them up in his hands. He pressed a small button in the wall next to the S-Gen unit and a drawer slid out from the wall. He dropped the towels and sheet inside, then gathered his discarded uniform and boots from the bathing room and dropped everything inside before closing it. A bright green light leaked from the edges of the drawer and I tilted my head to watch.

"That's the reclaiming unit. All matter is reduced to its base form and reused by the system."

I thought about it for a moment, looking around the room. There were no drawers for clothes, no boots on the floor, no half-eaten food on the small table next to the bed. "You use everything once and recycle it?"

He smiled. "Yes. The subatomic particles that made your towel might be used to create shoes tomorrow, or a bowl of soup the day after that. Everything onboard the ship is recycled this way. No one goes hungry. No one goes thirsty. No one suffers from poverty. As long as the ship has energy, we can create anything we need."

Holy freaking wow. I looked down at my new clothes. They were great, but I had one little problem. I'd worn leotards and other one-piece articles of clothing many times, and they were a complete pain in the ass when it came time to use the restroom.

Come to think of it, I hadn't seen a toilet in the bathing room. I looked around. There didn't appear to be one anywhere. I hadn't needed one yet, so it had slipped my mind. Which seemed weird, and wrong. Was there something wrong with me after all? Had the transport messed up my kidneys or something?

"What is it, mate? You can ask me anything." Dare lifted his hand to my cheek and I held still, allowing his touch. Already, he felt so familiar. Easier to deal with than Zane. But, for some reason, I was worried about the commander. He was so hard, so strong. He had so many people, a whole fleet of warriors, relying on his strength and I'd hurt his feelings. Little old me, Hannah Johnson, preschool teacher from Earth. I'd wounded the mighty commander with a few honest words.

Great. No toilet, and now I felt like a heartless bitch. This was just getting better and better. I sighed. I might as well ask Dare now, no matter how embarrassing it was to talk about. "I don't see a toilet."

Dare wrinkled his brow. "I don't understand, and my stims have no word for that. What do you need?"

Holy shit. Was I really going to have to explain it to him? I felt my cheeks grow hot, and this time it wasn't from arousal, it was just plain embarrassment. "You know, a place to go when you need to get rid of your body's natural waste? Don't you guys ever have to, you know, empty your bladder?"

Understanding dawned on his handsome face and he actually laughed at me, which both pissed me off and made my face feel even hotter. "Didn't Doctor Mordin explain this to you?"

"Explain what?"

"Everything is sent to the S-gen reclamation system. Even your body's biological waste."

"How?" What the hell was he talking about?

"Do you feel the need to empty your bladder?"

I thought about it for a moment, taking stock of how I felt. "No."

He smiled, looking relieved. "Good. You had me worried, mate. But it appears the implants placed during your medical exam are working properly."

"Implants?"

"Yes. During your processing, your internal waste systems were implanted with reclamation devices. This is done to our children at birth. The system will clean your blood, as well as transport and remove all waste from your body as it is generated."

Holy hell. I would never have to use the bathroom again? "So, I'll never have to—you know—ever?"

"Not unless you travel outside the range of the ship's system. If you were to explore a new world, and lose contact with our system, then your body's old biological processes would still function normally."

Weird. Not that I would miss that particular task, but I suddenly felt like an alien. Or a robot. Or something weird and not human. My hands were shaking a bit as I smoothed the front of my plain uniform.

"So the plug—"

"Can stay in as long as your mates see fit," he replied.

Time to think about something else.

The boring color of my clothing was better than being naked, but the basic brown and black pattern left something to be desired. I liked to wear bright red and blue and purple. I liked a flash of color. "Does everyone wear clothes like this?"

Dare tilted his head as if confused by the question. "Of course. Why would they not?"

I shrugged, not wanting to offend him, or his people. "Even the women? And the kids?"

He crossed his arms over his massive chest and frowned at me. "Yes. Does your clothing make you unhappy, Hannah? The uniform is designed to protect your body from extremes in temperature as well as protect you from wounds during an attack. The material is impenetrable, just like the armor of my uniform. Is this not how women dress on your world?"

I tugged at the end of my black sleeve where it settled against my wrist and tried to smile. Black. Every day. Forever.

Ugh.

"No, but I will adapt." My stomach chose that moment to grumble and I realized I was starving.

He stood staring at me as if I were an alien, which I realized more and more each moment, I was. At least to him.

"Come with me, mate. You need to eat, and I imagine you'd enjoy a tour of the ship? I have a few hours before I have to report for duty."

I worried my lower lip with my teeth. "You have to go out on a mission?"

"Yes."

"But why? I thought the ship was moving, heading back to the front lines."

"We are, Hannah. But my team flies scouting missions to make sure the fleet doesn't run into any surprises."

"Is it dangerous?"

His grin turned wolfish and utterly predatory. "I'm dangerous. And not just to my enemies, I hope." He leaned over and kissed the side of my neck, sending shivers racing over every inch of my skin. My collar heated and made my clit pulse.

No, not just to his enemies. Zane overwhelmed me, worried me, but Dare snuck under my defenses like a thief.

"I am hungry, and I would love to see the ship." Time to explore my new world, and find that damn transporter room. The way I felt about Zane and Dare already, I knew I needed to get off this ship as quickly as possible, before it was too late, before I fell head-over-heels in love with them. Zane wasn't happy with me. I'd felt that much. Leaving now was the best option. The question was, would I leave space with a training plug filling my ass?

CHAPTER EIGHT

Hannah

The dining hall was crowded when Dare and I entered. The space was small, designed to hold no more than a hundred people. About a dozen preschool aged children chased each other around the tables as their mothers sat, sipping steaming liquid from mugs. Scattered here and there at one of the long dining tables were small groups of warriors, most of them without collars. They smiled and allowed the young ones to climb on their laps and talk. Two mated males sat with their women—I could see now that they had matching colored collars—at one of the tables. One couple I noticed right away. My jaw dropped open and my heart raced with excitement. Dare tried to tug me toward a small, wall-mounted S-Gen unit, but I resisted his pull.

"She's human."

Dare looked over to where I was staring—I couldn't help myself—and he nodded. "Yes. That is Lady Hendry. The warrior seated across from her is her primary mate, Captain Hendry. He must be here to meet with the commander before we reach the front."

Dare tugged on my elbow again, and this time I followed him to the S-Gen unit in the wall. It was about the size of a microwave oven back home, and had the same black base and odd green gridlines as the one in Zane's quarters. My stomach growled again. I was starving.

"Place your finger over the activator like this." Dare pressed his thumb to a small indentation in the wall next to the machine. "And then just tell the ship what you want to eat." He ordered something I'd never heard of before, removed his thumb, and waited patiently as the inside of the box turned a bright green. When the light faded, a steaming plate of food waited for him, complete with a double-pronged fork and a knife. He removed his plate and turned to me. "Your turn."

"I don't know what to ask for." I truly didn't. I had no idea what any of their food looked or tasted like. All I really wanted was some of my mom's homemade lasagna and French bread.

He grinned. "The commander ordered a full menu from the processing centers on Earth when he found out you were coming. The ship is programmed with over two thousand menu items from your world. He wanted you to be happy here." This last he spoke with quiet sincerity, as if I'd doubt that Zane did it just for me.

I glanced at the other human woman and her mate. She had two adorable children with her. The older child, a sweet-looking little girl, looked like she was about four. Her younger brother was barely toddling around. Dare was watching me as I tried to make sense of the situation.

"Lady Hendry eats Earth food as well. But before you came to us, the menu from your home world consisted of a hundred items, and only from her country. Brides all over the Prillon system are celebrating your arrival. Deston is the highest ranking military officer still on active duty. No one else, except the Prime or Prince Nial, could have ordered the programming required to create this menu for you."

I tore my gaze from the happy couple and stared at the S-Gen. Here goes nothing. I placed my thumb on the activator switch. "Lasagna and French bread."

87

A kind female voice answered me, the voice of the ship's computer system, and I jumped in surprise. "Would you care for something to drink, Lady Deston? I sense that you are suffering from mild dehydration."

I *was* really thirsty. "How does it know that?" I looked at Dare.

"Your collar monitors your body's vital systems at all times. Once we claim you, the system will be able to help you maintain balance should you find yourself in need."

Shaking my head, I ordered a glass of water with lemon and turned back to Dare. "What does that even mean?"

He carried my plate and I followed him, sipping on the ice-cold water. It tasted like heaven. "It means, that if you are dehydrated or sick, the additional implants you will receive after we are mated will be able to transport water or other nutrients directly into your body's bloodstream, the same way it transports waste out of it."

I sat down in a soft brown chair and Dare sat down across from me. "Why do you guys even eat?"

"Because we enjoy it." He looked over my meal with curiosity before dipping his finger in the melted cheese and marinara sauce. He tasted it and took his time swirling the flavors around on his tongue. I watched him, curious as to what he would think of Earth food.

"Have you eaten food from Earth before?"

He nodded. "Yes, but only a couple of things. I have had your beer, and something called a hotdog." He made a face and shook his head. "That was not my favorite. But this?" He lifted his strange fork and cut a piece of my lasagna for himself. "This is fantastic."

I laughed at the look of astonishment on his face, like a little boy who'd just found a new toy. "Shall I go order one for you?"

He smiled, but before he could answer someone walked up to stand beside us. I glanced over to find the human woman with long blond hair staring at my plate as if she'd never seen lasagna before. Her voice was melodic and reminded me of my music teacher in high school.

"Oh, my God. Is that what I think it is?" Her mate stood behind her with a bemused expression on his face. Their young daughter was in his arms, her hands wrapped around his neck and a look of utter contentment on her face. I knew that feeling; I'd had it when Zane held me in almost the exact same position. The little boy was clinging to his mother's leg.

"If you think it's lasagna, then yes."

Her eyes sparkled with delight and she clapped her hands in front of her face with excitement. "Yes! I've been stuck eating mac and cheese for five years! You must be Lady Deston." She held out her hand and I shook it.

"I'm Hannah."

"Anne." Her gaze held mine and I knew, at least in part, what she was feeling. It was nice to see someone from home. I remembered Warden Egara's words, that I had been the first volunteer from Earth. I had to assume that Anne had been a prisoner. I wondered what she had done to be convicted and sent off-planet. As soon as I considered that, I realized that her punishment *was* going off-planet. She didn't have to dislike it. In fact, by looking at her with her mate and children, she was quite happy.

"Nice to meet you."

"Up, mama." The little one held up his pudgy little arms and I stared at the boy in wonder. He didn't look as fierce as the warrior who was his father, but he was still not exactly human either. The little girl's eyes matched the warrior who held her, and I assumed he was her father. But the little boy? He looked slightly different, with greenish eyes and a different tone to his skin. Was the boy a child of Anne's second mate? Did she have a second mate? Didn't all Prillon brides? But then, I had two mates, and I was only with Dare at the moment. Perhaps her other mate was off flying a spaceship or something.

I had no idea, and there was no way I was going to ask. Both of the children were adorable, and all of a sudden I could imagine myself with a couple of babies of my own, one with Zane's amber eyes, and one with Dare's gray ones.

"You have beautiful children." I smiled at her as she leaned over to pick up her son. My compliment was an honest one.

"Thank you." Our gazes locked, and I knew I had made a friend. "What did you do, on Earth I mean?"

No one had asked me that, and the normal conversation felt good. "I was a preschool teacher."

"Wow. You must have the patience of a saint. I was a nurse."

Blood. Guts. Mucus. Yuck. "Wow. I couldn't do that. I see blood and I pass out."

"To each their own." We both chuckled, but her mate interrupted us.

"I'm sorry, my love, we must go. We must return to our ship. I have a meeting in an hour." The giant male spoke for the first time and my entire body tensed. I knew that voice. Oh, my God, did I know that voice—asking if I accepted his claim—placing his giant hand around my neck and pulling my naked body back against his massive chest as another man, his second, feasted on my pussy—

The memories flooded me with heat and I had to look down at my plate, hoping my stupid body would just calm down and leave me alone. But no such luck, as he spoke directly to me this time with that deep voice. "Welcome to you, Lady Deston. May you find every happiness with us as a bride of Prillon."

My answer was more a squeak than true words. "Thank you."

Anne reached out to touch my arm and I felt like I had to look at her again, or risk being very, very rude. When I looked up into her blue eyes, I could see that she knew what I'd seen, what I'd experienced in the bride processing protocols. She *knew*. I could see it in her eyes as her mate's large hand came to rest on the side of her hip. Her next words confirmed it. "The processing protocol?"

I couldn't look her in the eye and lie. I just couldn't. "Yes. I'm sorry."

She threw her head back and laughed out loud, the sound one of utter delight. I froze, shocked at her reaction. I'd expected her to be angry or embarrassed. Instead she couldn't keep the smile off her face. "You're welcome, *Lady Deston*." She placed a heavy emphasis on my new title. "You're very, very welcome."

I felt my eyes widen and she winked at me as her mate gently pulled her toward the door. She looked back over her shoulder. "We are going to be great friends, Hannah. I'll see you again, soon."

I waved as she left and turned to find Dare studying me, his nostrils flaring as if he could smell my arousal. Then I remembered that he could, in fact, *feel* it through our connection. A guilty blush crept up my neck and face, and I knew I was turning a bright pink. I'd liked… no, loved, what Captain Hendry and his second had done to Anne. I craved that kind of dominance.

"Explain, Hannah."

I shook my head, refusing to tell the man my true feelings, and took my first bite of lasagna instead. The flavor of tomato and oregano, mozzarella cheese and thick noodles exploded on my tongue. It was the best lasagna I'd ever tasted. I made a small sound of pleasure and hurried to take another bite, my stomach suddenly an empty, aching cavern.

Dare watched me for a moment, then decided to let the matter drop, eating his own food quickly.

When we were both finished eating, a kind-faced Prillon woman walked to our table and took our plates with a shy smile. I thanked her, and she bowed to me. "My pleasure, Lady Deston. Welcome. May you find much joy among us."

"Thank you." I looked up to discover that everyone who was still in the dining hall, which was eight unmated warriors, six small children with their mothers, and one mated couple who appeared to be in their sixties were all watching us openly. I turned to Dare, suddenly uncomfortable to be the center of attention. "Why are they all looking at me?"

His chest was puffed up with pride, and his smile one a man gives when he is feeling generous and all too pleased with himself. "They are waiting to meet their new lady. The commander is second in line to the Prime on our home world."

I had no idea what a Prime was, and my confusion must have shown on my face.

"The ruler of our planet. Our king."

Holy shit. Deston was third in line for the throne of his whole freaking planet? I felt my chest get tight. Hot. It was hot in here.

I looked from the approaching couple to Dare, who appeared to be enjoying my moment of panic, because he continued. "Zane, my cousin, is also the most feared warrior on the front. He is the commander of the entire coalition fleet, not just this battleship and its battle group. You are Commander Deston's bride, Hannah. And the second highest ranking member of our entire fleet."

"What? What does that even mean?" I whispered the question in a hurry, as the elder warrior and his bride were already approaching the table. I didn't know anything about war, or battleships, or their enemy. I knew how to wipe noses, sing 'Wheels on the Bus,' and paint the alphabet with watercolors.

Dare leaned back in his chair and crossed his arms over his chest, nodding almost imperceptibly to the male headed toward me. "The Prime rules our planet, but the commander rules all of the coalition military forces. He has more real power and influence than the Prime, because he oversees warriors from all member worlds. Zane rules this region of space. On Earth, Hannah, I believe you would be called a queen."

For the next hour I was introduced to and greeted by everyone in the room. I couldn't complain. They were friendly, warm, and seemed genuinely happy to meet me. I tried to smile and make small talk, but the truth was, with my stomach full and the day's events wearing me down, I was getting tired. Dare watched me like a hawk, and the moment the last chubby little hand had held mine, he stood.

"Thank you all for your kindness to Lady Deston, but she is weary from her transport. I must take her back to our quarters now for some much-needed rest."

They all nodded agreement and Dare wrapped his arm around my waist and led me from the room in almost the exact same way Captain Hendry had led Anne. He towered over me, but he didn't remove his hand as we walked the hallway back to our quarters.

The walls shifted from a dark orange, to blue, then back to the familiar cream-colored brown that I knew meant we were close to our private quarters. As we approached, my thoughts turned to Zane. He was in charge of the entire outer space army, the same army that protected Earth and all the member worlds? He was the leader of all of it?

And more important, would he be in our quarters, waiting for me? What was I going to be dealing with when those doors opened and I stepped inside?

Dare must have felt the muscles along my spine tense as we drew nearer.

"The commander will be on the command deck all night. We arrive at the front soon. I have a few hours before I must report for duty. He will return for you then. We will always care for you, Hannah. You will never be alone or unprotected, not while we live."

"Yes, but you might *die*. Both of you. I can't give myself to a man—to two men—who willingly put their lives in danger."

"You are a bride of Prillon, Hannah. To be sent here means you are like us, you seek the harsh edges of life, Hannah. You enjoy a sharp bite of fear or pain, that hint of danger."

I remembered the dream and the hand about my throat.

It hadn't been real, but I'd *felt* it. I'd liked it, being tied down, submitting to not one man but two, his power over me evident in the way he touched me.

"I see by the flush on your cheeks that you admit this is true." When I was about to speak, he held up his hand, tucked a finger around his collar. "You can't hide it. Perhaps Zane may choose to deny it as well, for fear of hurting you, but I can see it clearly. You were matched to Prillon because of our prowess, in bed and in battle. If we weren't warriors, you wouldn't want us. You must relent and trust in the match."

"Yes, but…" I began, but bit my lip.

Dare cocked his head. "What?"

I tugged at my collar. "I sense… I sense he's holding back."

Dare's eyebrows went up at that. "He's commander. He has many secrets."

The answer was vague, but probably true. Was I feeling a wall so that Zane didn't share the horrors of his job? It was a worthy question, so I just nodded in reply. I would need time to consider and, perhaps, more time with Zane.

"Now then," Dare said, coming up beside me, stroking his knuckles over my cheek. "Both of your mates need not be present to continue your training. No Zane tonight, just me."

I hated myself a little bit as my entire body relaxed at the news. Zane was so big, so intense, and so damn hard to resist. The connection with him was even more powerful than with Dare. I didn't want to deal with my fears where he was concerned, for that strong connection also meant strong fear that I would disappoint him. That idea is what tore me up inside.

Was I drawn to Zane because he was a warrior? It made no sense, for all my experience with men on earth made me run from their false dominance. I had learned the hard way that, more often than not, their concerns had always been selfish ones. With warriors of Prillon Prime, however, I knew what I felt through the collar could not be faked.

I didn't want to deal with my emotions where Zane was concerned. They were still too raw. A yawn threatened to escape me, but Dare's next words ruined the soft, contented feeling.

"We only have a few weeks to prepare you for the claiming, and I am not the kind of warrior to neglect my mate."

CHAPTER NINE

Hannah

Dare opened the door to our quarters and waited for me to precede him into the room. The moment the door slid closed, my gentle and considerate companion disappeared.

"I know Zane is being careful with you."

I turned to him and frowned. So, Zane *had* been holding back? I'd felt it, through our connection, but having Dare confirm it made me feel uneasy. It was hard to believe because the fucking, God, the fucking, had been incredible. What else did Zane want from me that I hadn't given him? What else did he need from me? I'd given them everything. I'd given him everything—but my heart. That was still my own. "Why would Zane—I mean...?"

"Zane believes you are too soft, too small to take our cocks the way we want to fuck you." Dare leaned over and tipped my chin up with his fingers. "I will not be so soft, mate. I need your body prepared for me." He kissed me then, softly, so sweetly that his words took an extra moment to register. "I do not want to wait any longer than necessary to claim what is mine."

I thought back to our time together with Zane. Was I confusing pleasure and power? Had Zane treated me like something fragile? Something that would break? And if he had, would I be able to withstand more if that's what he needed? Would I break, as he feared? Would he give me the chance to test my own limits? Did I want him to?

The thought made my pussy clench. God, yes, I wanted him to push me. I wanted to feel completely owned. I wanted to trust Zane to know just how far he *could* push me. I wanted to close my eyes and surrender to him. But I didn't dare, not yet. I could feel the darkness riding him. He was afraid of something. Afraid he would hurt me? Or afraid he would break me? "Am I really so small, compared to your women?"

Dare lifted my arms over my head and held them there, staring down into my eyes. "Yes, you are small."

"So is Anne. And she seems just fine with Captain Hendry."

Dare chuckled. "She is at least half a head taller than you are, little one. With a rounder ass and wider shoulders."

True. Anne was at least six inches taller than I was, but I was average on Earth. And not small by any measure. According to my doctor, I needed to lose at least thirty pounds. I lowered my arms to cover my rounded abdomen, ashamed. Is that why Zane held back? Was I too big? Too soft? Too—

"Arms up, Hannah, as if you are trying to reach the ceiling." By the deep tone of Dare's voice as he stared at my chest, I knew the sight of my breasts pushed forward had captured his complete attention. Well, at least being a little heavy did have the advantage of larger breasts.

I stood still, not sure what to do, but his commanding tone sent a wave of electricity over my skin. Was I allowed to be with Dare without Zane? I didn't know. What was I supposed to do?

Slowly, I raised my arms. "Are we supposed to—I mean—without Zane?"

"I am your second, Hannah. Your collar is around my neck, and I accepted your claim."

"I didn't—"

"Do you reject the connection between us? Do you refuse me as your second?" Dare stepped in front of me until my face was so close to his massive chest that I could see nothing but him. "Would you deny me, mate, and demand Zane name another?"

My pussy clenched at his tone. I liked this more dominant side of him. "No." I had no idea if I could force the issue or not, but I didn't want another mate, or a different second. Zane was *mine*, I knew it deep in my bones, even if he didn't feel the same.

But Dare? He was already claiming a piece of my heart. And while I needed another dominant, controlling male like I needed a hole in my head, I craved it. Just the sharp bite of Dare's words had my pussy wet.

Dare crushed his lips to mine, his long tongue teasing and tasting me as if he would never get enough.

I felt his huge hands reach up and around me to the back of my neck. One tug on the uniform I wore and the top half of it split down my back.

"Oh!"

He peeled it from my body slowly, leaving my mouth to kiss his way along every inch of bared flesh as he undressed me. Shoulders, arms, breasts, belly, and thighs all felt the swirl of his tongue. When he knelt down to pull the clothing off over my feet, I stood before him naked and quivering. My weariness from earlier was gone, swiftly replaced by pulsing desire.

"Lie down on the bed. I want you on your stomach, Hannah, and wait for me there while I select another training plug."

I walked to the bed and clenched down on the one that was still deep inside me as I crawled onto the silky coverings. The dark red material felt like satin under my palms as I made my way to the center of the bed and lay down. Dare took his sweet time selecting a plug, and when he turned to face me, I saw that he had the next larger size in one hand,

and a small bottle of lubricant in the other. Our gazes locked as he closed the distance between us and my pussy clenched at the lust I saw in his eyes.

He was beside me before I could recover my equilibrium and he placed the large plug on the small of my back so I could feel the weight and breadth of it.

"Spread your legs, Hannah. Let me see what's mine." When I was too slow to comply he landed a sharp smack on my bare bottom. The sting spread like wildfire on my still sore cheek and I bit the bedding to keep from crying out. I inched my legs a bit farther apart, but Dare, apparently tired of waiting, shifted and used both hands to force my knees wide. Reaching over my head, he removed a large pillow from the head of the bed and lifted my hips to place the pillow beneath me. The anal plug fell beside me, but Dare wasn't paying attention to where it landed, not with my body open, his playground.

Now I was completely at his mercy as he knelt behind me, between my legs. My ass was up in the air, on perfect display. Surely he could see the base of the smallest plug settled against my stretching entrance. My pussy was open as well, the air in the room a cool reminder that he could see—everything.

"So pretty, Hannah. So tight. Zane's seed drips from you." Dare rubbed my ass cheeks with both hands, pulling hard enough to spread my pussy open and put a small sting in my virgin hole. His fingers swiped through the wetness coating my pussy and spread it about. It heated and tingled everywhere it touched, arousing me quickly.

Carefully, he took hold of the plug in my ass and tugged on it, working it from my body. I sighed as my body relaxed, feeling inexplicably empty. Dare picked up the new plug.

"Dare, I don't think—I'm not ready—" The second anal plug was too big, too long, just too much.

Two large fingers were shoved into my pussy and I cried out at the invasion. "You were saying, mate?" He finger fucked me until I moaned and pushed back against his hand.

"Not ready? When your pussy is so wet I could fuck you right now, take you hard and fast and you'd beg me for more?"

He continued to torment me with one hand, but the other lifted the bottle of lube to my ass. I felt the small invasion as the pointed top entered me, then the warm flood of the liquid as it coated my insides. Soon I would be filled there with an even larger device than last time.

"I've only been here a few hours." My voice was breathy as he continued to work both my holes. "Surely I need more time to adjust to the small plug before you use a new one?"

One of Dare's fingers circled my back entrance. I flushed, knowing it wasn't as tight as it had been; the plug had done its job.

"Your entire body is readying itself for the claiming ceremony, Hannah. Even your ass is adjusting, readying. Your body would eventually change to take us both on its own, but the trainers will speed the process. I can tell you are ready for the next size. I would not harm you. Trust me."

After he put the next sized plug in, would Dare then fuck me? Would he put his huge cock in my pussy and make me his, as Zane had already done?

When he pulled the lube from my ass, he removed his fingers from my pussy and I had to clench the bedding with tight fists to stop myself from begging for more.

"I'm not going to be gentle this time, little mate. You are ready, and you will take what I give you." With those words, he spread me with one hand, and inserted the tip of the anal plug with the other. "Why? Because I know you want it."

"Yes!" I cried at his rough actions.

He didn't hurt me, but he wasn't gentle, as Zane had been. He twisted the device and pulled on my ass until I couldn't deny him. I felt the moment my muscles popped free and the plug slid in deep and fast in a rush of pleasure-pain that tore a moan from my throat. When it was fully seated, Dare pulled back and forth on the plug gently, not fucking me with it, but teasing me with the possibility, until

I felt like begging him to do something more. Anything more.

His released the device and I panted, waiting and wondering what would happen next.

His hand landed on my ass with a sharp sting and I yelped.

"That was for lying to me, to yourself, Hannah. You *were* ready. You were more than ready."

That was true. It had gone in with surprising ease. While it had stretched me, it did not burn and I wasn't even sore.

"I'm sorry." I didn't care what I had to say, I needed to come. I needed him to make me come.

"You're sorry? Aren't you forgetting something?" He pushed two fingers back inside my pussy at the same time as his other hand landed with a sharp sting on my other cheek.

Forgetting? God, what was I forgetting? "What?" I cried.

He struck again, a little harder as his thumb found my clit and pressed down a little too hard. I needed stimulation to have an orgasm, not this constant pressure. I wiggled my hips, trying to force him to move, and his hand struck again. "Hannah, when we are in our private quarters, you will call me master or sir. Do you understand?"

"Yes."

In a move so fast I didn't see him change position, I was flipped onto my back and he loomed over me. He watched my face as he worked me with his whole hand, bringing me to the brink again and again, then leaving me just as the wave of a release was about to break through me. Over and over until I was thrashing on the bed, nearly in tears. "Do you want to come, Hannah?"

"Yes."

"Yes, what?" His hand stilled and I opened my eyes to stare up into his dark gray gaze. His lust was feeding mine through the collars, and I couldn't even imagine what he must be sensing from me. Was this connection how he knew just when to stop? I was strung so tight I felt like I

GRACE GOODWIN

was going to explode.

"Yes, sir. Please."

His smile was almost enough to make me come, right there. I'd pleased him, and the warm feeling flooding my chest had nothing to do with sex and everything to do with making him happy.

Dare lowered his mouth to mine and stroked me over with his tongue in my mouth mimicking the movements of his hand below. When I screamed, my whole body lifting from the bed with the force of my release, he stole my air, then kissed his way down my body to take my pussy with his mouth. He sucked and licked my clit, using his fingers to stroke me inside until I shattered again.

"You see, Hannah, your submission does not come with a painful price. When you give it freely, you will receive only pleasure in return. There is no need for your fear. We aren't like the men on Earth."

He rose then, and shed his clothes to stand at the edge of the bed. He pointed to the floor at his feet. "Kneel, Hannah."

I felt like melted wax, but I crawled to him already eager to taste the pre-cum I could see beading on the head of his giant cock. I knelt before him, and the pleasure I saw on his face made my heart feel like it was about to burst from my chest. Anything he wanted. I'd do anything. I would submit, for I knew he would only give me pleasure. I needed to please him in return, needed him to be happy with me. These Prillon men fed my sickness in a way no human man ever had. I didn't just want to pleasure my master; Dare's happiness had somehow become my own. I wanted to see the same dark look, feel the same bite of command from Zane as well. I didn't think, though, that that would happen.

I didn't want to think about that right now, not with Dare's cock inches from my lips. I knelt on my knees with my legs open and my hands resting on top of my thighs, palms up. I was ready to do whatever he asked, be whatever he needed me to be.

102

"Fuck me with your mouth, Hannah, until I come down your throat. Swallow me down. All of me. Now."

I leaned forward eagerly and sucked him. I worked him with my tongue and stroked his balls and the base of his cock until he buried his fingers in my hair and lost control. I could barely breathe, but I didn't care. His pre-cum spread inside my mouth, heating my blood to a fever pitch that threatened to send me into another orgasm. I devoured him and took him deep, until there was no room for air, and I held him there for as long as I could, the pressure building inside me, the need for oxygen growing within me. I knew he could feel it through our link, and I knew it was making him wild.

"Oh, mate, how you tempt me." He pulled back and I sucked in a ragged breath before sucking him hard and fast. He came, his cock jerking in my mouth like a wild animal as I drank him down. I came at the first splash of seed against my throat, my body heating and softening, clenching down on the thick rod in my ass.

As soon as he was done, he sank to his knees in front of me and reached for my pussy. He bent me back until my shoulder blades hit the side of the bed and my neck arched backward. My head rested on the bed as he towered over me, his mouth on mine and his hand moving hard and fast in and out of my pussy, stroking my clit to make me come again.

It only took a few seconds before I shattered into pieces. He held me in place, pinned between the bed and his large body. When my pussy stopped pulsing around his fingers, he kept me there, his hand deep inside me and his mouth on mine. His kissed changed from demanding to gentle, his touch from aggressive to tender and I had no will to do anything but stay where he wanted me, to allow him to worship and calm me after the storm.

When his lips left mine to follow the path of my neck, I didn't move. I couldn't. I had nothing left.

"Hannah, sweet Hannah."

"Yes, sir?" My response was more sigh than anything else. My knees were hurting and my bottom stung, but I couldn't move, not so long as he wanted me here.

"You will sleep now."

"You don't want… you don't want to fuck my pussy?" I whispered.

He slowly shook his head, but I could see his eyes narrow with desire. "Your pussy is for your mate to fuck until you are bred. Only when Zane's seed has taken root can I fuck you there. Until then, I have other ways to bring us both our pleasure." He shifted me. "For now, sleep."

That sounded good to me.

Dare lifted me from the floor and pulled back the bedding before placing me inside like a little girl. I wondered if he planned to leave me, but sighed with contentment when he slid in beside me and covered us both. I curled into his side, safe and warm and content, and I trusted Dare to watch over me as I slept.

CHAPTER TEN

Zane—Three weeks later

I returned to my quarters after another long and troublesome night reviewing the reports coming in from the front. We'd arrived at the battle zone more than a week earlier but the Hive was gaining ground. We'd lost two small freighters and one scout ship so far, but after months of zero losses, the shift in enemy tactics was not good news for my fleet.

And the news from my private life was not much better.

I was not winning the war for my bride's heart.

Hannah had been mine for three weeks now. Dare had somehow calmed her down about her concerns for our lives, but something else lingered. She still had not vowed to accept my claim. I was running out of time. And, as usual, when I returned to my bed it was to find her wrapped around Dare, both of them naked and sated, and pressed together as if they were already one flesh and one mind. And I was not part of that equation.

I could feel her pleasure from Dare's touch from as far away as the command deck. Our bond through the collars was a constant reminder of her pleasure—without me.

Hannah would not look at me, not the way she looked

at Dare. She was supposed to be *my* match. *Mine.* Yet she turned to him, trusted him, wrapped her naked arms around him and slept.

I *wanted* her to accept him as her second. I needed her to accept him, but a dark and angry part of me twisted on the inside when I saw them together like this, when I wanted and couldn't have her affections. I needed her in a deeper, darker way than what she could handle and my frustration with not taking what I needed from her made me blunt and too curt with her, which sent her running back to Dare. It was more powerful with the collars.

With me she was constantly nervous, fidgeting and biting her bottom lip because she could sense I was... off. She seldom looked me in the eye, and rarely laughed if I was in the room. Dare spent more time with her than I did, my role as commander keeping me away from her much more than I liked.

I understood the logical reasons why she would feel more comfortable with him. He was more affectionate. He touched her in little ways, smiled at her, and constantly brought her gifts. Me? I wanted to pin her back to the wall and fuck her like a wild animal. I wanted to tie her to my bed and force orgasms from her beautiful body until she broke from the pleasure, until she ceased to think and could only feel what I gave her. I wanted to spank, paddle, and flog her perfect ass as I controlled her body, her orgasms, her very pleasure. Until she lost herself completely and forgot her own name, but not mine. I would have one name fall from her lips, when nothing else mattered to her: *master.*

As commander, I needed an outlet, a release for the stress and yet I knew it couldn't come at the price of her body. I was beginning to doubt the matching process. She was supposed to be perfect for me, but she was fragile and so small. The things I wanted would just scare her more, so I held back. I tried to be more like Dare. Softer with her. Tender. Careful not to scare her. And it wasn't working. It wasn't fucking working.

I'd decided to seek outside guidance. Enough was enough. I needed an expert, and in my fleet, when it came to human women, there was only one.

A snooze alarm sounded and Dare's eyes opened instantly. His gaze settled on me at once. His reflexes were as sharp as ever, which was one of the reasons I trusted him to keep my Hannah safe.

"Zane."

I nodded and looked at Hannah's dark hair where it rested nestled in the crook of his arm. I ached to reach out and stroke the silky strands, especially now when she was asleep. She wouldn't be withdrawn or resistant if she wasn't awake. "How is she?"

"I told you, she senses something with you. The collar allows her to feel your rejection."

My eyebrows went up. "I'm not rejecting her!" I tried to keep my voice low, but it was difficult.

"You aren't showing all of yourself and she knows it. You're frustrated with her lack of acceptance, but how can she accept you when she *knows* you're holding back? Growling at her all the time isn't going to help us win our claim." Dare's voice was barely more than a whisper, and I lowered mine to match. Neither one of us wanted her awake for this conversation.

This was also the first time Dare had spoken to me about Hannah's feelings and I crossed my arms. Was my caution with her that obvious? "All right, second. Tell me what you need to tell me. My matched mate is afraid of me. What else do I need to know?"

Dare rolled his eyes and I wanted to punch him. "She's afraid of loving you. She's afraid one of us is going to die, of course, but besides that, she knows you aren't giving her everything when she's practically bared her soul."

"That's life for a Prillon bride."

"You are such a hard ass, Zane. Was your head diamond hard when your mother gave birth to you? Or did you grow into it?" Dare sighed and gently moved our sleeping mate off his shoulder. She was dead to the world, as she was most mornings. Not an early riser, my Hannah.

My second slid from the bed and I grit my teeth as I saw that they were both very naked. I enjoyed fucking my mate, but she did not curl around me and sleep as she did with Dare. I wanted that trust from her. I needed it with a ferocity that was eating me alive, burning in my gut like acid devouring my flesh from the inside.

Dare used the S-Gen to summon a clean uniform and put it on. He was due on the flight deck in less than an hour. I was sending his unit to scout the enemy base that had been reported on the fifth planet's moon in the system. If the reports were true, the Hive was expanding their territory again. Which was bad news for everyone.

Dressed and ready, Dare stopped before me and placed his hand on my shoulder. "Look, Zane, you need to talk to her more. She lost her parents when she was young. Her brother was a weakling and a parasite, and the men of her world took advantage of her submissive nature. They used her. The master she trusted to care for her used her up like a selfish child and hurt her, badly."

"This is exactly why I can't let her see my baser side. If she's this fearful of me now, imagine what it would be like if she knew the truth."

Dare slowly shook his head. "You're pushing her away and she's doing the same. Both of you are stubborn. Perhaps you should trust in the matching protocols. Maybe she wants you just as you are."

I looked from Dare's pleading gaze to the beautiful and very fragile female in my bed. "Doubtful," I grumbled. She wouldn't want me if she knew the truth of my ways. "She has told me none of her secrets—about these men." I spat out the last word as if it were distasteful. Anyone who used a woman as Dare described was not a *real* man.

"You haven't asked." Dare slapped me on the shoulder and turned to leave me alone with my mate, but I felt the need to warn him.

"Prince Nial is going out on patrol with you."

Dare rolled his eyes. "Again? Seriously, Zane, when are you going to send that spoiled little playboy home?"

"Explain yourself." I knew my shoulders had stiffened up, but Dare was throwing caution to the wind this day, speaking his mind about more than just our mate.

"He's reckless, Zane. He takes too many chances. It's like he thinks he's invisible to the Hive. I've had to cover his ass more than once."

I chuckled. Yes, my cousin, Prince Nial, was all that and more. "He's young, Dare. Were we not invincible once as well?"

Dare shrugged. "Don't blame me if he gets his ass killed."

"Noted." Dare left me alone with my bride and I stared down at her with hunger for her touch gnawing at me from the inside.

I thought about taking off my clothing and climbing in beside her, but she would startle when she woke, and that beautiful pink blush would make its way from her chest to her delicate face. I knew, because I'd already tried it, more than once. If I wanted to fuck her, she would let me, and she'd be hot and wild and responsive in my arms. When we were done, and I'd wrung every drop of pleasure from her body, she would turn away from me and get dressed, claim she needed to be in class.

Dare had arranged for her to work with the young ones on board the ship. She had transformed them, bringing songs and games from Earth to our children. The little ones loved her as I did, and her eyes glowed with happiness when she was surrounded by their youth and innocence.

When I watched her with them in the surveillance room, my heart actually hurt, as if she'd stabbed me with a knife and left the blade embedded. I watched her often, feeling like a foolish stalker and not her chosen match.

I definitely needed expert help.

Decision made, I gently shook Hannah's shoulder and

woke my bride. I watched her move, studying the soft lines of her curves, enjoying her grace as she dressed. Once she was covered, I took her to the transporter station. Captain Hendry and his bride were expecting us. Anne was human, from Earth. Hendry was her matched mate. If anyone could help me figure out what to do with Hannah, it was he.

In the transporter station, I took Hannah's hand and led her up to the transportation platform. She spun around, looking at the floor.

"Where are the little circles?"

"There are no circles." She was talking nonsense, but her confused look was so beautiful, I couldn't resist stealing a kiss. When I was done with her, she was panting, and I could smell her arousal, feel it burn her up through our link, but she pulled out of my arms and turned in a circle, looking from the floor to the ceiling and back again. Over and over. "Hannah, hold still so we can initiate the transport."

"But where are the circles? How am I supposed to know where to stand?"

"My mate, there are no circles."

"But, isn't it like *Star Trek*? You know, stand in the circles and *'Beam me up, Scotty'*?" Her pulse raced and I could feel her unease.

I stepped closer and pulled her against my chest, wrapping my arms around her to hold her in place. I used my hand to hold her cheek over my heart. "Hush, mate. There are no circles on the floor. Just hold still. I've got you." I nodded at the transport engineer and felt the odd wrenching and twisting for a few moments that meant we were traveling from my battleship to Captain Hendry's smaller cruiser.

Hannah was trembling in my arms and when I looked down at her face, I saw that her eyes were closed. "Hannah, you can open your eyes. It's over."

"Wow. I was asleep last time. That felt like riding the down side of a rollercoaster that never stops."

"What is a rollercoaster?" I wanted to know her, to

understand her, but it was like she was speaking another language, like she was from another world. Which she was. My heart felt heavy with the thought, but I didn't have time to dwell on it.

"Welcome, commander! Lady Deston." Captain Hendry and his mate stood at the edge of the transport.

Hannah turned in my arms and I let her go. "Anne!" The women hugged and Anne pulled out of Hannah's arms with a warm smile. "Come, Hannah. I want to show you around. I've heard so much about you from my daughter. She loves you already." The women exited the room and I watched Hannah until the door slid closed behind the women.

"I assume my mate will be protected on board your ship, captain?"

He grinned at me. "Two of my best men will be three steps behind them."

"Good." I stepped from the platform and we greeted each other in the way of warriors, our forearms pressed together as our arms locked in friendship. "Now, where's the alcohol?"

Hendry laughed at me. "Drink all you want, commander, it won't do you any good. My ship will simply pull the poison from your blood as fast as you can drink it."

I sighed. Sometimes, I really hated technology. I remembered the days of my youth, when I could actually drink myself into a stupor. "I know. Damn it anyway."

He thumped me on the shoulder. "Come on. Let's go somewhere we can talk about that pretty little mate of yours."

I followed him to the command deck of his ship, then inside the small, attached war room very similar to mine. We were alone.

"Talk to me, Zane. What the hell has you so desperate you've come over here to ask me for advice?"

As uncomfortable as this conversation made me feel, it was the reason I'd come to this ship. I needed help winning my Hannah's heart, and no matter how gentle and considerate I tried to be with her, no matter how much pleasure I gave her, she kept her heart from me. "She is my match. I saw the reports myself. Nearly one hundred percent compatibility. But she chooses my second, and turns away from me. She is afraid of me. Dare says she senses I am holding back. She never lets down her guard. I know I scare her, but the more I try to rein myself in, the worse it gets."

Hendry sat down at the head of the meeting table and watched me as I paced the room. "And what else does Dare have to say about it?"

"That she lost her parents and was poorly used by men on her world. Dare says I need to talk to her more, to tell her about my more dominant ways."

As an old and trusted friend, he knew of my baser proclivities. He had them too.

Hendry crossed his arms and leaned back, watching me. "But you decide for her what she needs or doesn't need?"

I ran my hands through my hair with a growl. "I don't know what she needs. Nothing feels right. She's so small! I have never met another human, other than your Anne. I don't know their culture or their customs. I fear I will break her."

Hendry chuckled. "May I speak freely, commander?"

I slumped down in the chair next to him. "Please. Tell me how to deal with these human females."

Hendry chuckled. "Hannah's not the problem, Zane. You are."

"What?"

"You're the one who is holding back. You are the one rejecting your mate."

I opened my mouth to deny his bullshit, but he lifted his hand. "Hear me out."

"Make it good, Hendry, or I might decide to gut you and walk away." The captain raised a brow, but didn't rise to the bait. We'd been friends for many years, and I honestly wanted to hear what he had to say.

"She's your match, Zane. Yours. What does that mean?"

"I don't know, and I'm going to lose her in less than a week if I don't figure it out."

"Do you remember my claiming ceremony?"

Oh, yes. I remembered. He'd fucked Anne hard and fast, both he and his second rutting into her like wild animals as she'd whimpered and screamed and begged them both for more. I'd been one of his inner circle, one of those lucky enough to witness the claiming and pledge my life and sword to their joining.

Hendry looked me dead in the eye. "I fucked Anne. My second took her as I restrained her, as I spanked her bare ass. We shared her body like two wild animals. I held her throat and I tied her down and I fucked her until she couldn't remember her own name."

I cleared my throat. Fuck me. I wanted to do all that to Hannah. All that and more. "Yes. I was there."

"But that wasn't the first time." Hendry leaned forward, his gaze intent. "Your Hannah was matched to Prillon Prime, to *you*, using the recording from Anne's NPU. Your Hannah experienced that claiming for herself." The captain placed both of his palms flat on the table, as if he were trying to anchor himself for what he had to say next. "Hannah lived that, from Anne's point of view. And that experience is what drew her to you. Don't be tender, Zane. Stop holding back. She's a submissive, and she's sensitive to your needs. She knows you're not giving all of yourself. She can sense it the same way you know she's unhappy and uncomfortable around you. But she doesn't know what you want her to be, Zane. She needs you to be who you truly are; she needs to know the rules. She won't give herself to you, she won't love you, she won't trust you until you bare your soul to her and let out the beast."

CHAPTER ELEVEN

Hannah

Zane was oddly quiet as we walked back to the transporter room. I looked up at him from the corner of my eye, but looked away when his gaze turned to me. Something was different. He was calm, eerily calm, as if Captain Hendry had given him a tranquilizer or something.

Hell, maybe my mate just didn't really like my company. I'd given up trying to talk to him after the first few days. He was the king of monosyllabic responses, and I got sick of trying to pry information from him that he obviously didn't want to give.

He fucked me every night as I took Dare in my mouth. They'd explained to me that only the primary mate was allowed to deposit seed in my pussy until I was pregnant with my first child. After that, my body was a free-for-all and both men could take me as hard and as often as they liked.

I knew that first night, when I said I wanted to go home to Earth, that I'd pushed Zane away, that I'd disappointed him. I regretted hurting him, but no matter how hard I tried to please him, he wouldn't let me in. Since that first night, something wasn't right between us. I felt the chasm

114

growing, like a partial tear that kept ripping a bit wider each day. He was cold and hard, and while he still looked at me with desire, took me with a desperate need, there was also anger. The collar, while able to share the immense pleasure between the three of us when fucking, also shared other powerful emotions as well.

Where had the caring man I'd met in the medical station gone? Where was that mate? The one who bossed me around one minute and treated me like spun glass the next? The mate who held me down and suckled my nipples as the doctor made me come, then held me on his lap and rubbed my back to make me feel like I was safe. Where was the mate who had held me over his lap, spanked me until I cried, and then promised me that I'd never feel alone again? Where was my anchor in the storm? My master?

He was gone, and I was afraid I'd never get him back. I had grown to love Dare, I knew that, but being with Zane like this, walking beside each other in the corridor, not touching, not talking, not feeling anything from him but an impenetrable wall of ice? I couldn't do that. Not for the rest of my life. I wanted more. I deserved more.

I hadn't told Dare yet, but I had decided to seek a new match when the thirty days was over. Dare would be upset with me, and I would miss him, but I didn't see an alternative. That meant I had four days left with my mates and then I'd move on and give Zane the freedom he so obviously wanted. I would not be his fuck toy, the woman he refused to speak with during the day, but would stick his cock in every night. I refused to love Zane, knowing he would never love me in return.

And even when we were together, the three of us, Zane fucked like a perfect clinician, but I could tell he was holding back. He wasn't fully there with us, and I was tired of feeling like such a disappointment to him. Zane was not happy with me, and his pain hurt me. I needed to make my mate happy. I needed to be what he wanted, what he needed. And I was a complete and utter failure there. Zane was miserable, and his pain was breaking me. I had to leave so he could find a mate he wanted, a woman who satisfied him, a woman with whom he would share his darkness instead of hide it.

Maybe I would be sent to another battle fleet, as far away from Dare and Zane as possible? Could I ask the bride program here to send me away from Zane? I was heartsick, but seeing my mates every day would be so much worse.

I didn't know what requesting a new mate entailed, but I intended to ask. Maybe, when Prince Nial went back to their planet in a few days, I'd go with him. Surely they could assign a new mate for me there? And I'd never see Zane or Dare again.

The thought felt like a knife blade in my gut, but I couldn't live like this. I'd failed my mate. I wasn't what he wanted or needed. It was time to let go.

We stepped onto the transport platform and Zane pulled me into his arms once more as the strange pulling and twisting feeling moved through me. When it was over, I expected Zane to release me, as he had before. Instead, he looked at the transport engineer over my head. "Transport us to my private quarters on deck seventeen."

"Sir?" The engineer hesitated and I stiffened in Zane's arms. What the heck was on deck seventeen?

"That's an order."

"Yes, sir."

I wrapped my arms around Zane's waist and hung on as the transport took us from the platform to somewhere new, a place I'd never heard of before. When the transfer was complete, I tried to step out of Zane's embrace and look around, but he didn't allow it. He lifted me and walked me backward until my back bumped into a soft wall. Zane lowered his hands to where mine were on his waist, took hold of my wrists and raised them above my head.

"I've been keeping something from you, my mate. I believe you've sensed it these past weeks."

My pulse raced as he stretched me up and up until I stood on tiptoes. "What?"

"Me."

I felt something cold and hard as steel clicked into place around my wrists. Zane's grip loosened and I tried to lower my arms, but couldn't. I was trapped.

My pussy clenched and I shuddered at the heat in Zane's eyes as he dragged his hands slowly down the insides of my raised arms to cup my breasts through the fabric of my tunic. He pinched my nipples hard, and I gasped as his mouth lowered to mine.

His kiss wiped my mind of all thoughts but him. His long tongue curled and explored, taking and tasting as his hands ripped my clothing from my body. When the kiss ended, I was naked, my clothes lay in shreds at our feet, and my pussy was so wet I could feel my arousal coating the tops of my thighs in welcome for his huge cock.

Zane's forehead rested on mind, and his hands were now on the curve of my bare hips. "You will call me master. Nothing else."

I shuddered, so afraid to want him this much. I didn't hesitate in my answer. "Yes, master."

He kissed my cheeks, then my chin. "If you need me to stop, say lemonade."

What? "I hate lemonade."

"I know, Hannah. I know. I read your file. Memorized it, in fact." His mouth closed over my nipple and I moaned as the tugging sensation sent currents of lust straight from my breast to my clit. He'd memorized my bride file? In the bride processing center I'd spent four full days answering endless questions on everything from my favorite food to childhood memories. They even had my school test scores all the way back to first grade.

"Zane."

He nipped at my breast just hard enough to hurt. "Master."

How had I forgotten, stretched out like a pagan offering with my hands locked over my head and my naked body his for the taking. The room was deep red, like his collar, with a large bed on one side and the toy table opposite. I was tied to a hook that protruded from the padded wall. Hooks and straps of various sizes and shapes hung from at least a dozen places on the wall. The two near my feet were easy to figure. They were obviously meant for my ankles. But the rest? I had no idea.

I'd read about something like this in my romance books on Earth. A dungeon. It was what those who were into the BDSM lifestyle used to play sexual games. For sex. For fucking.

"Master, why? Why didn't you tell me? I thought you—"

He undressed as my voice trailed off. I watched him as he revealed the hulking size of his shoulders and huge chest. His body slanted down in the perfect V shape, complete with defined abs and a cock big enough to make me faint.

My ass was empty for the first time in days, having taken the largest sized plug with ease and not needing them any longer. I didn't know what I wanted more, his cock in my empty pussy, or taking me for the first time in my ass.

God, I wanted both. He walked away from me to a small table that lined the wall. On it was a variety of plugs and dildos, ties, and things he could use on me. How? I had no idea.

I didn't have any more time to wonder as Zane returned and knelt on the floor at my feet, a large dildo in one hand and lube in the other. I expected him to turn me around and get my ass ready for the dildo; instead he locked his mouth over my clit and sucked until my eyes closed and my knees buckled.

When I was on the edge, he pushed the dildo up inside my pussy in one fast, hard stroke, stretching me wide as I exploded all over his mouth.

Using the back of his hand, he wiped my dripping desire from his mouth. "I know you fear I will die in battle. I do not fear death, mate; my only fear was afraid that I would hurt you, that my rough and aggressive ways would scare you away. You are so small, so dainty and fragile. I hid my true self from you. No longer."

"This was why you rejected me?" I felt sadness mingled with hope.

"Reject you? Never. I was protecting you. From me. From my dark ways."

I saw the truth in his eyes, felt it pure and strong through the collar.

"I want your dark ways," I admitted. "I need them. I need all of you."

He looked up at me and simply nodded.

Panting and out of breath, I didn't resist when he turned me around to face the wall. My pussy was still stuffed full of the dildo. As expected, I felt the tip of the now familiar lube enter my back entrance, and the warmth of it spread inside me in a wave. Instead of feeling a plug at my ass, I felt nothing until Zane lifted me off my feet.

He unhooked my arms from the wall above me and carried me in front of him to the edge of the bed where he settled me on my knees. As soon as I'd gained my balance, his hand wrapped around my throat, softly, gently, and I arched back as the memories of Anne's claiming flooded me and his hard chest pressed to my back. Yes. I wanted this.

"Do not move, mate, or I will have to discipline you."

I couldn't speak, my voice completely gone as I waited, breathless for the inferno of power I felt building in him. He wasn't holding back. This was Zane, the *real* Zane. *Finally.*

He pulled my hands behind me and wrapped them with soft but unbreakable bonds, forcing my breasts to jut out. The ties were snug, but not too tight and I gasped as a blindfold descended to cover my eyes.

"To heighten your senses, and of course to wonder what I will do to you next."

My breath came in short spurts but I was ready and eager for him to take me, to own me. I was near tears, and I didn't understand how the salty fluid had found its way to my eyes.

119

I wasn't in pain, but I felt like I was about to explode into a hundred pieces of broken glass and only Zane could hold me together.

Just like I remembered from the bride protocol simulation, Zane's heated flesh pressed to my back and his deep, commanding voice filled my ear. "Will you accept my claim, mate? Or do you wish to name another primary mate?"

Zane's voice was thick with lust, and the explosion of his need blasted through my collar like a blowtorch. I'd never felt this, never felt *him*. At last he was letting me in, showing me what he needed me to be, what he would truly give me.

"I—" Words failed me. I couldn't say yes. Not yet. What if he stopped? What if this was just some sort of sick and twisted game to fool me into accepting him and Dare—and then he'd go back to his old ways? I had to know where he would take me. I needed to know if I could trust him, or if he was just going to use me like the others, but never show me his true self.

When I fell silent, he growled in my ear.

"Very well. I understand. I feel your doubt, Hannah. I earned that mistrust by not being honest with you about my needs." His hands slid down to cup my breasts and I moaned. He pinched them hard, and my moan turned to a sob as the stimulation flooded my system. I pressed my ass back against his cock, trying to force him to take me, to end my loneliness.

"No." He stepped back and I swayed on my knees as his voice circled me. "Tell me what you need, Hannah."

"I don't know."

His hand was suddenly at the back of my neck, forcing my face to the bed. Ass in the air, he held me there as I squirmed, fighting his hold with my hands locked at the small of my back. One hard strike on my naked ass and the first tear fell from my eyes to soak the dark red satin.

"Tell me what you want." His hand rubbed the tender spot where he'd just struck me. "But don't forget to address me properly, mate. What do you call me?"

"Master."

"Very good." One hand at the back of my head, the other he moved to spear my ass with two rough fingers. I cried out as he spoke again. "Tell me what you want."

"I don't know, master." It was a lie, a bald-faced, full-out lie, but I didn't trust him, not yet. Not. Yet.

"Oh, my sweet little mate. You're lying to me." I shuddered as he finger fucked my slick and well trained ass. He lifted his hand from my head and stood. A few seconds later I felt totally empty as he slid his fingers from my ass and left me on the bed with my arms tied behind me and my ass up in the air. "Do not move, mate, or your punishment will be much, much worse."

Frowning, I tried to imagine what his punishment would be, but was quickly distracted by something solid on the inside of my right ankle. A heavy strap was tied around it. Once that was secure, Zane moved to my left side and pulled my legs wider, strapping something between my ankles.

Oh, shit. A spreader bar. I couldn't close my legs, couldn't kick or fight or squirm. The idea flooded my pussy with heat and made my breasts achy and heavy where they hung down. I couldn't see Zane, but I could hear him moving around the room. The anticipation, not knowing what was coming next made me force the air in and out of my lungs in short bursts.

With no warning, Zane lifted my hips and slid some kind of hard cushion beneath them that lifted me enough to take most of the weight off my knees. I wouldn't be able to lie flat or pull away from him. I tried to bend my knees, to lift my feet a bit, but discovered that they were tied down.

I'd never been this vulnerable before. Ever. My heart raced as panic started to form in a cold, dark pit in my gut. What if he hurt me? What if I wanted to get up, needed to get away, and he wouldn't allow it? What if he fucked me and left me here for hours, or days? Would the alien technology in my body keep me alive if he left me here?

They were stupid thoughts. Zane had never been anything but courteous and caring. Demanding and curt, but never cruel. But that didn't matter right now, not to my heart or my body, both of which were working themselves into a full on panic.

God, what was my safeword? The word that would make it all stop?

Lemonade. Did I want to stop him now? I'd asked for this and he hadn't hurt me, not yet. If I stopped him, then what? Then what?

I wanted him to—God, I didn't know. I didn't know. I didn't know what to do or think or feel. I squirmed on the cushion, tried to roll over so I could move. I needed—

"Do not move, mate. Not one inch, or you will feel the sting of my crop."

And just that fast the panic left me and I froze in place, grateful that he had taken the choice from me. He placed one huge hand on my hip and traced the curve of my ass and hip, my waist and shoulder as he made his way to my hands. With a soft tug he secured them a couple of inches above my spine, forcing my shoulders down into the bedding if I didn't want to wrench my shoulders out of place. I could stay like this for a long time, but not if I fought, not if I tried to lift up off the bed.

I was well and truly trapped now, and so fucking hot for him I could barely think. The dildo stretching my pussy was big, but it wasn't moving, just torturing me with what I didn't have—his cock pounding in and out of me.

He took his time running his hands over my skin, making me tingle and want. I let him pet me, my body completely his as I reveled in his exploration. He could take whatever he wanted now, do whatever he wanted to my body, hurt me, fuck me, love me, make me scream with pleasure—and that scared the shit out of me. But it also made me hotter than I'd ever been in my life.

"Now, Hannah, tell me what you want."

I shook my head as his fingers circled my virgin ass. I wanted everything, but I was too afraid to admit it. What if he thought I was a freak for liking a little pain with my pleasure? What if he was like my ex-boyfriend on Earth, the man who'd smacked my bare ass and then laughed as if my need to feel safe and restrained by my lover's command was some kind of joke? I couldn't stand it if Zane laughed at me, or thought I was sick, or some kind of freak. I couldn't.

"Hannah, answer me now."

"I don't know, master."

His sigh made my pussy walls clench and I squeezed my eyes shut behind the blindfold, afraid I'd made him angry.

"Lying to me isn't allowed, little one. Now you must be punished."

I heard soft footsteps as he made his way to the table lined with sexual apparatus, then came back to me. The only warning I had was his command. "You will count, Hannah. One to ten as I strike. If you do not count, I will continue until you remember to do so. Do you understand?"

Oh, shit. Count what?

A soft whistle sound filled the air just as a hard object struck me on the bare bottom, driving the dildo deeper into my pussy and making fire spread over my bare cheeks in a fierce burn. I bit my lower lip and clenched my jaw as raw heat spread over my ass, down my thighs, and around to my clit.

He struck again and I whimpered. Again. *Crack.*

My ass was on fire before I remembered to count.

"Five."

"No, love. That's not the number I told you to start with." *Crack.*

I whimpered as he hit the back of first one thigh, then the other; the pain took me over and spread through my body like warm honey in my bloodstream. *This* was what I'd feared, this feeling of floating, of existing for his pleasure, of being lost in sensation. Of opening the door to the darkest parts of my soul with a mate who didn't want me, didn't understand—

"Count, mate." His rough voice dragged me back to the room, to him. I wanted to please him. I needed to please him. I needed to be what he wanted me to be. I needed to be his. I needed—

Crack.

"One, master." I counted to seven as he struck again and again, all over my ass and thighs. It was some kind of paddle, hard and unforgiving. Tears soaked my blindfold but I didn't feel them. They were from a secret place inside me that I kept locked, a dark reservoir of pain and fear that I held inside me all the time like a cancer. My needs ate at me because I tried to lock them away, hold them down, and smother them like a beast. I was the monster. This darkness in me was what I didn't trust anyone to see, what I didn't trust Zane to see. I needed the pain he was giving me to unlock the monster's cage. I needed him to break me so I could let the darkness out, so I could stop fighting it and let go.

Crack.

The dominant male behind me drove on and on as I stopped counting at eight and let the fire take me, let the tears stream. I didn't want to worry about Zane or Dare dying, or the secrets Zane had been hiding from me. I didn't want to miss Earth's blue skies and green grass and the feeling of warm sunshine on my face. I didn't want to be Hannah; I just wanted to be *his*.

The spanking stopped but I didn't move, content to float and let him take me wherever he needed me to go.

"Hannah, you stopped counting."

I didn't respond. Did he require a response? The bed dipped with his weight and he lifted my face from the bed. I could smell his pre-cum as his cock danced over my lips. The chemical in the fluid raced through my bloodstream, waking me up with streaks of lightning shooting straight to my clit.

He stroked the side of my face with the back of his hand

as he shoved his huge cock into my mouth. "Suck my cock, Hannah. Suck me down as I finish your punishment. If you won't count, as you were told, I will use your mouth for other pleasures."

I opened my mouth and wrapped my tongue around his huge cock as he fucked my mouth and brought the paddle down on my ass. His pre-cum and the burn of the spanking made me writhe and moan, completely lost to the world. Only he existed. His cock. His fire making my bare ass burn. I was close, so close to an orgasm that I wanted to beg, to scream, to plead with him to let me have release. Instead, he plunged in and out of my mouth in a relentless rhythm that forced me to fight for air.

His cock swelled and pulsed in my mouth, his cum coating my throat and roaring through my body to my clit. I clenched and pulsed around the dildo still stretching me wide as my pussy fluttered in the first stages of release. But his hard hand grabbed my hair and lifted me off him with a harsh pull that stung and the orgasm stopped just before I exploded.

"Now, mate, tell me what you want."

I tried to hold back, but he'd broken through all my barriers. He knew exactly what I needed. He knew how far to push me and still be safe enough from me using my safeword. He *knew* me. My soul was naked and I didn't have the will to lie. I licked my lips, trying to draw the last of his essence into my mouth. "You, master. I want you to spank me until I forget myself and float away. I want you to fuck me until I can't walk. I want you to make my body burn until I scream and come all over your cock."

He traced my lower lip as I whispered the broken words, my dark confession. No more hiding, no more worrying. Just my master and me.

"Good girl. Don't ever hide from me again, mate. Do you understand?"

"Yes, master."

"I want to give that to you, Hannah. I *need* to give that

to you. This is why we were matched, because we will give each other exactly what we need. These past three weeks, oh, Hannah, what we have been fighting. No longer."

Zane left my side. He removed the pillow from under my hips and moved into position behind me. I felt his cock nudge my back entrance and I tried to push back, to rock my hips into him. "Do you accept my right to you, Hannah? Do you accept my claim as your primary mate?"

"Yes. Yes. *Please*, master." I needed him to fill me up, to take me.

"Now I will fuck you until you scream."

"Yes, master." If my hands had been free, I would have twisted them in the sheets. But I was bound, my ass in the air, my legs spread wide by a hard bar. All I could do was accept whatever he chose to give me.

I needed him to be the first in my virgin ass. I needed to *belong* to Zane. I loved Dare, but Dare wasn't my master. Dare was my lover and my friend, my second. He made me feel safe and cherished. He was easy to please, easy to make happy. But his darkness wasn't part of his soul. Zane forced me to yield, he took my pain and released it, forced me to let go, to submit. Zane *needed* me to surrender. He craved my surrender as much as I needed to feel free and safe in his dominant embrace.

With the dildo stretching my pussy, Zane pushed forward slowly into my virgin ass, breaching my trained ring of muscle, pushing past easily and filling me to the brink of pain. When he was fully seated, balls deep, I was panting, and clenching down on the rod in my pussy as hard as I could. I needed to come. I needed—

Zane's hand landed on my ass hard, and I jerked forward, pulling myself almost off his cock. He soothed the sting with his palm. "Good girl, now push back and take me again."

I tried, but when I didn't take him fast enough, Zane buried his fist in my hair and pulled back, forcing my body to open wider, faster. The sting of pain on my head made me shake. The fire on my ass spread into a hot glow and I wanted more, needed more. In an act of defiance I knew he would not let pass, I struggled against the bonds the held my wrists. If I could just get one hand free to stroke my own clit. There! I was almost free. Maybe, if I hurried, I could come before he stopped—

Smack.

He struck my bare bottom again and used his hold in my hair to shove me forward. "Bad girl, Hannah. You don't have permission to use your hands."

"I'm sorry, master." God, just calling him master made my pussy get even wetter. I was so close, I couldn't think straight.

"Come back here, Hannah." He aligned the broad head of his cock with my back entrance once again. "Fuck me with that ass."

I shifted back, again not fast enough, and he yanked on my hair, pulling me back hard and fast and slamming his cock deep. I groaned at the roughness of his actions, the intense feel of him filling me completely. It was painful, but I needed it. I needed that bite of pain, knowing he was there with me, giving it to me. He was bigger than any of the training plugs. Hotter, thicker. His pre-cum coated my walls and made my arousal even more intense. I wouldn't be able to take much more. He fucked me in earnest then, holding my hair for leverage and pulling me back or holding me in place, depending on his need. My moans of pleasure turned into whimpers of desperation as he drove me higher and higher, filling me up and making me his, totally and completely, at last.

His cock swelled inside me and I knew he was close. He freed my hands and they fell to the bed beside me. The burn in my shoulders made me moan as more sensation clouded my mind.

"Up, Hannah. Up straight. Reach behind you and lock your hands around my neck."

I straightened up off the bed without thinking, settling

myself back until my thighs met his own, still impaled on his rigid shaft. His chest was pressed against my back.

The position arched my back and shifted his cock to press forward, pushing the dildo inside my pussy harder.

"Don't move, Hannah."

"Yes, master." The threat, his absolute control let me be free, mindless. His. I was his.

I held him, my back to his chest, his cock in my ass and my hands in his hair as he whispered in my ear.

"Come for me, Hannah. Come for me."

He slid his hands down over my stomach toward my pussy. His arms were so long, so strong, and I was so small in his embrace that he could easily reach both my clit and the rod filling my pussy.

Cock still in my ass, he fucked me with the rod and stroked my clit until I shattered. I screamed his name, again and again. My body exploded with pleasure, but I was more spun up each time, almost as if each orgasm was just a warm-up for the next one. I was lost on a sea of sensation, crying out helplessly, giving him everything and holding onto him for dear life. His hair in my fists and his words in my ear my only connection to the real world.

You're so beautiful. I don't know why I resisted so long. You love it like this. You love it rough, taking my cock into that virgin ass. You will love being filled with two cocks. Soon enough, Hannah, it will be Dare filling you as well. We will fuck you together, without mercy.

His words became muted by my cries of pleasure. When I was spent, he finally let himself come, filling my ass with hot seed and the power of his cum, the chemical overload set me off again.

We both collapsed on the bed and he pulled out of me slowly before removing the other object from my pussy. That done, he rolled me to face him and kissed me softly, gently, over and over until all the emotions of the past few weeks rose up like a tidal wave and I sobbed.

He kissed me again, his hand resting on my cheek as if I were the most precious thing in the universe. He pulled the blindfold from my eyes and I looked at him. His eyes were dark amber and flooded with a need so raw and powerful that I gasped.

"I'm sorry, Hannah. I'm so sorry."

I stared into those eyes and I froze, afraid to move, afraid I'd lose him again as he removed the spreader bar from my ankles and climbed onto the bed with me. His voice was ragged and deep as he pulled me close. "I almost ruined this. I was afraid you wouldn't want me like this."

I blinked at him, confused. "Like what?"

"Out of control. So hungry for your body that I would push you too far, ride you too hard. I was afraid I would hurt you, Hannah. Or scare you away."

"I'm not afraid of you, not like this." I closed my eyes and nuzzled the hand he rested on my cheek. "I was afraid of you before. Afraid I couldn't make you happy. Afraid you would never let me see the real you. Afraid to want you like this. Afraid you didn't really want me."

He tensed, and I opened my eyes to see that his lips had thinned and his brows were drawn together. "You are perfect, Hannah. I want you. I need you. I need to take care of you, and push you, and make sure you're safe. I see you with Dare and I see your trust. I need that, Hannah. I need you to give me everything."

"I just did."

He shook his head and moved his hand from my face to trace my bottom lip. "Not your heart, Hannah. You didn't give me your heart."

He looked so sad, so broken, that I had to do something. I couldn't stand to see him in so much pain. His anguish was mine. He hurt, and I hurt. "Master. You've showed me what's been missing, what you need. What *I* need." I leaned forward and pressed my lips to his, trying to ease him, trying to take the hurt. I loved him. At least, I thought I did. But I couldn't say the words. Not yet. Not right now.

Not when he hadn't said them first. I wasn't doing that again, not ever. I'd told my last serious boyfriend that I loved him, and he'd used me for my apartment and my money, cheated on me and dumped me when the next best thing came along.

Zane was, admittedly, nothing like that idiot boyfriend, but he was still a man who wanted me, who needed me, who loved to dominate me in bed—and who didn't love me.

I kissed him again because I didn't know what else to do. He rolled on top of me, already hard, and I welcome him like this, soft and slow and tender. I opened my legs and he nudged my entrance with his cock. With a sigh, I let him in.

As hard as he'd been before, he was gentle now. He kissed me, slow and sweet and soft on my lips as I lifted my hips to meet him. I wrapped my arms around his head and made sure he knew I wanted him with me, like this. Always. And after he spilled his seed inside me, I held him close. I ran my fingers through his hair and soothed the lines from his brow, more at peace than I'd been since leaving him. I held him with all the love I could not speak, and we slept.

CHAPTER TWELVE

Zane

I sat in the children's classroom and watched my beautiful mate charm the little ones. They sat in a circle on the floor, sang songs and clapped as she smiled at them with such light in her eyes that I knew she loved them all. And she loved me. I could see it in her shy smile, and the warmth behind those dark brown eyes. Her gaze would soften when she looked at me now, and I could feel her joy and acceptance through our link.

She loved me, but she would not speak the words.

I wanted her to admit her feelings. I needed to hear them. At our claiming ceremony tomorrow, I had every intention of forcing the issue.

A toddling youngster made her way toward me, her big eyes happy and soft gurgling noises coming from her sweet little body as she inspected my boots. Children were rare on the battleships. Only the high-ranking officers, those lucky enough to have mates, had families onboard. The children transported to the battleship each day for schooling, and for safety. We were the largest ship in the battle group, and the children's rooms were housed in a specially reinforced and detachable escape vessel.

The young girl placed one chubby little hand on my knee as she tugged at my boot with the other. A few weeks ago, I would have tolerated the little one's attention, but left feeling uneasy. The children were so small, so fragile and innocent. I never felt comfortable around them before, but something had shifted within me last night, something profound. For the first time in my life I was at peace. I had shown my matched mate my darkness, and she'd not only accepted me, she'd ridden through the storm of my passions and wrapped her small body around mine, twining our legs together as we slept.

I had her trust at last, and I'd never worked so hard for a prize, or valued it more.

The child before me shifted her attention from my boot to my face and she lifted her arms to me. "Up."

With a frown, I leaned down and lifted the tiny creature into my lap. She patted my face with her chubby fingers and stared up at me with a very serious expression on her sweet face. "Mander."

I had no idea what the child was saying, but Hannah rose from her seat on the floor and walked over to rescue me.

"Yes, he's the commander, isn't he?"

The tiny girl nodded her head as if she'd been asked the most serious question in the world. Then she leaned forward and kissed me with a big, wet, open-mouthed kiss that landed somewhere between my bottom lip and my chin. I froze, utterly at a loss, and Hannah laughed out loud, the melodic sound of her joy worth the slobber that now coated my face.

The girl patted my cheek, as if to let me know she was done with me before wiggling her bottom to let me know she wanted to be set down on the floor.

My hands covered her entire body as I placed her gently on her feet. She waddled away and I looked up to find my mate smiling down at me. Hannah stepped between my legs and lifted a hand to my chin with a smile, wiping the wetness off with her thumb. "Your people love you, *mander*. Every single one of them."

"Not all, my mate. Not the one who matters most to me." I looked at my bride and imagined her body swelling with my child, with a sweet little girl who would give me sloppy, wet kisses, or a strong young boy who would challenge me and make me proud. I wanted my seed growing in her body. I wanted to know that she was mine in every way.

She blushed a beautiful shade of pink as I held her gaze, the color not quite as dark as the deep pink that took over her skin when she came all over my hard cock, but a sweeter, softer color. I wanted her to say I was wrong, that she did indeed love me. Instead, she smiled that secretive female smile and leaned over to kiss me on the mouth.

I would accept that, for now. Until the claiming, which was scheduled to occur just hours from now. But there was a problem. A serious problem that I had not shared with her; something that could ruin this fragile new bond between us.

I was here with her in the children's area awaiting bad news. I did not want my mate to be alone when the scouts' reports came back.

Reaching out, I grabbed her hand and nodded to the other two women working in the room. "May I borrow my mate, ladies? I would like to show her the command deck."

"Of course, commander." The senior instructor, an elderly woman who had been mated to one of my best engineers for many years smiled at us both with real warmth. Hannah was right; the people in my fleet looked upon me with a warmth I'd never noticed before. My mate had opened my eyes to their respect and trust. The weight of command had never felt heavier, but it had also never been as much an honor as it was now and for the first time in my life, I smiled at the woman.

"Thank you, Lady Breenan." I enjoyed the older woman's flush of genuine pleasure at my words and pulled Hannah out of the room and into the hallway. "Come, mate.

I will show you where I run the ship."

Hannah sighed happily and walked with her hand in mine and her cheek pressed to my shoulder. Her contentment buzzed through my collar, making me heady with satisfaction. There was no better feeling than knowing I'd cared for my mate and made her happy, content, and at peace. Well, maybe feeling her pleasure take her when I fucked her senseless, but I didn't want to think about that right now. I would not walk onto the command deck with my cock hard as iron ore. And not when I knew her happiness could evaporate at any moment.

Dare was missing. And Prince Nial. We'd lost contact with them several hours ago and I was waiting for news from a recon team that was due back at any moment. The decision to keep this from her was a difficult one, but she'd know the truth soon enough. I just hoped my second was still alive.

As if fate had heard my thoughts, the communications officer's voice filled the hallway. "Commander, the recon team is back. They are waiting."

"On my way." I knew from the tone of his voice that the news was bad. Hannah must have sensed it, too. She stiffened and lifted her head from my shoulder.

"What is going on, Zane?"

Squeezing her fingers, I pulled her into a transport tube and entered the code that would get us access to the command deck. "Dare and Prince Nial were shot down by Hive forces a few hours ago. I sent a recon team to scout their location for and extraction."

"Oh, my God. Is he dead? No. No!" She tried to pull away from me as the transport slid to a stop and she swayed with the rapid change in direction. She crashed into my chest and I wrapped my arms tightly around her. Her pupils dilated and she was breathing too quickly, short shallow panting that would make her faint. "You knew and you didn't tell me! You knew! How could you sit there and play with that little girl and smile while you knew?"

Hannah pounded at my chest with her fist and I grabbed it, holding her still, locking her in place. I stared down into her gaze until she calmed. "I know you love Dare, sweet one. I will get him back for you. You have my word."

Her dark, expressive eyes filled with tears, but she turned her face away from me to bury her head in my chest. "Promise me, Zane. Promise me."

"My sacred vow, mate. Dare will be back onboard this ship in time for us both to claim you." Which didn't give me much time, but that was for the best. If the Hive had Dare and Nial, my warriors would not be faring well. The Hive liked to torture biological life forms before transforming them into something more machine than man. The process took several days, and I could not allow them to have my best friend, or the Prime heir.

I took Hannah onto the command deck, where warriors stopped what they were doing long enough to bow before their *Lady Deston* and pay their respects. My mate made me proud, holding her head high and keeping the worry from her face. She fooled them all with her bravery, but I could feel her fear through our link. My mate truly was my match and perfect for me in every way; passionate in sexual play, she needed the release my mastery gave her but could walk with her head held high as a queen's when faced with pain and danger. My respect for her grew, and my love. I would sacrifice an entire fleet if it meant keeping her safe, and that was a frightening admission.

I had to get Dare back. If I failed, not only would I lose my friend and cousin, but I'd have to find another second that my sweet, stubborn Hannah would accept. And judging by the fire in her eyes as the scouts gave their report on the Hive, she would have no other second but Dare.

"We'll leave within the hour and I'll lead the extraction team myself." My second in command opened his mouth to protest, as he should, but I didn't allow him to speak. "I promised Lady Deston I would have Dare, her second, back to her in time for the claiming ceremony tomorrow, and that is what I will do."

"Yes, commander." I left them all behind as I escorted Hannah back to our quarters. Once we arrived, I pulled her into my arms for a kiss meant to drive all thought from her mind.

"You will remain in here until I come back with Dare. You will remain locked safely behind this door until I come for you. Do you understand?" I held her face in my hands and stared into her eyes to make sure she was listening to me.

"Yes."

"Yes, what?"

She lifted her hands to my arms and wrapped her fingers around my forearms. Turning her head, she kissed the inside of my wrist. "Yes, master. I will stay here, safe and sound, so you can bring Dare back to us."

I kissed her hard and left without another word. The recon team was waiting for me when I got to the launch bay. We were going in on three ships, a team of eight on each. The recon team had tracked Dare and Nial to a small mobile Hive station recently discovered on a nearby asteroid. The outpost was small, and not capable of holding more than a hundred Hive soldiers.

With the taste of Hannah on my tongue, I knew I could kill a hundred Hive alone.

I was an excellent pilot, but the pilots chosen were from the recon team and knew exactly where we needed to go, so I sat in the back with the other warriors and waited. Battle fever spiked my blood with energy and I smiled, eager to kill. I hadn't tasted battle in months, and was eager to feel my enemies' bodies rip and tear as I pulled them to pieces with my bare hands.

"Hive communications have been blocked," the pilot yelled back to us where I sat with six other warriors in eager silence. "We'll be on the ground in sixty seconds."

I pulled the breathing mask from the wall behind me and suited up for battle as the others around me did the same.

The ship landed and I followed the recon team out the door. In less than five minutes we were setting charges on their outer perimeter door.

The blast sounded and the explosives team motioned the rest of us forward. We moved like water over rock, in perfect harmony. These were my warriors, my team, and we had fought alongside each other for years.

Hive soldiers flowed through the opening like swarming insects and we picked them off easily from our vantage point in the rocky terrain surrounding their mobile outpost. The Hive soldiers were well programmed for direct conflict, but one-on-one, or in small groups, they couldn't adapt fast enough. The Hive was stupid, but their robotic soldiers came off the production lines on their home world faster than we could destroy them.

In a matter of minutes, the flurry of activity was over and my warriors and I made our way to the entrance. If this was a normal Hive outpost, the expendable robotic units would have been sent to flood the perimeter while the more advanced biological hybrids would be inside waiting to ambush us.

I threw a gas canister through the blast hole in the door and we waited long enough for it to have knocked out their biological systems. The gas wouldn't kill them, just knock them out. We had our own warriors trapped inside, so could not use lethal toxins.

We cleared the outpost one room at a time. There were no biological to be found until we got to the very center of the structure. There, lying on two tables in a medical station were Dare and Nial. The half-living, half-machine creatures standing over them were the only resistance left. A warrior on my right stunned the creature over Dare as another team took care of the creature over Nial.

I stepped forward and looked down at my second, at Hannah's love, then a war cry left my throat as I lifted the semi-conscious creature from the ground and ripped his head from his shoulders with my bare hands.

CHAPTER THIRTEEN

Hannah

Zane was back. I could feel him again, and Dare. But not with warmth or any kind of joy. They both felt cold, Dare just absent, and Zane?

Zane felt like pure, raw fury.

I rubbed at my neck and paced the confining space of our quarters. I couldn't stand to look at the bed where I'd slept so many nights wrapped around Dare. Nor could I look at the lounge where my mates had first taken me, Zane's strong hand at my back and Dare's pre-cum on my lips making me dizzy with lust.

I paced, happy that I could feel them again, even if it wasn't warm and fuzzy.

Five minutes passed. Ten. And still Zane didn't come for me. My collar had gone cold and lifeless when Zane left the ship. At that moment I realized just how connected I'd become to my two warriors, how much I depended on that constant link to feel like I belonged to them, like this was home.

I'd very nearly told Zane I loved him today, but I was firm on this. I had given my warriors everything else—my trust, my body, my soul. I would not give them the words first. That was the one thing I demanded they give me, and I would not relent, no matter how Dare flattered and teased me, or Zane pushed me to the edge and brought me back safely in his arms. I would not yield. Not on this.

But if Zane didn't come for me soon, I would disobey him. I could tell by the buzzing numbness in my connection to Dare that something wasn't right. And I would bet they had taken him to the medical station. Doctor Mordin was probably looking at him right now, making sure he was okay.

The door to our quarters made a dinging sound and I ran for the door. *Finally!*

I unlocked the door, expecting to see Zane in the hallway.

Instead, a weapon was pressed to my chest and the old man who'd stared at me like a lecherous toad in the medical station when I first arrived smiled down at me. I'd since learned his name was Harbart, and he was Prince Nial's future father-in-law, or whatever they called it here.

I felt sorry for Prince Nial. If Harbart's daughter was anything like her father, the poor girl had to be a horrible creature.

"Lady Deston. I need you to come with me." His eyes were cold and hard and he pressed the tip of his weapon exactly between my full breasts. I didn't know exactly how good this armored clothing was, and I didn't want to test it.

"I can't. I'm sorry. Commander Zane ordered me to stay in here until he returned." I was stalling, and we both knew it. The cruel tilt of his smirk made me shiver and I took a step back trying to get the pointed space weapon off my body. I had no idea what the strange weapon could do, but I had no desire to find out.

Harbart followed me into the room and sealed the door behind us before turning back around to face me. I stared up at him in horror. He was huge, like all Prillon warriors. I barely reached his shoulder, and he probably weighed twice as much as I. His blank expression had transformed, from cold and unfeeling to that of a monster. His lips peeled back to reveal his teeth, his dark yellow eyes were wide and wild, and one hand curved around the weapon, the other curled in the air as he raised it to strike me, the gnarled fingers like a withered old tree branch.

He hit me hard across the cheek and I staggered backward, landing on my ass on the floor. Pain sliced through my skull but I welcomed it, knowing Zane would feel it, knowing he would come. I swallowed the bile rising in my throat and tried to think of a way to survive long enough for Zane to get here.

"You cunt whore." Harbart stepped forward and I scrambled backward like a crab on all four legs, but I wasn't fast enough and his kick connected with my hip. I rolled into a ball on my side, in complete agony as he leaned over me with spittle on his chin. "Nial was supposed to die today. And you? You aren't supposed to be here at all. Zane is mine."

He kicked at me again but I was waiting for it. I grabbed his leg and pulled with all my might. I managed to get him off balance and he fell backward with his arms flailing like windmills.

Gasping for air, I tried to stand, but it felt like I had a knife in the side of my hip. The pain flooded me, but I knew how to deal with pain. Pain woke me up. Pain made me feel alive. And this asshole was after my mate. I had no idea what this monster wanted with Zane, but I wasn't going to let him get it.

Half crawling, half staggering, I headed for the S-Gen in the corner of the room. If I could get there, maybe I could ask for a baseball bat, or a golf club. Something! I'd never fired a gun in my life, and I doubted the ship's systems had been programmed for human weapons.

Reaching the platform, I stretched to place my hand on

the activation panel—

"Don't move, Hannah Johnson of Earth. Or I will splatter your brain all over the wall."

Zane

I paced the medical station and waited for Doctor Mordin to complete the examinations. We'd been back on the ship for nearly an hour, and I could feel my Hannah's impatience building. But I wouldn't go to her without answers.

"Well, doctor? Can you save them?" Dare was covered in superficial Hive devices, thin metallic modifications they'd made to his skin and eyes. But Nial? The bastards had obviously started their work on the prince first.

"Dare will be fine, but I'm not sure I can remove the implant from his right eye. It will enhance his vision, but isn't dangerous long term."

I released a breath I hadn't realized I'd been holding. So, my second would have a metallic glint in his eye for the rest of his life. But he would be alive, and whole, and *himself.* Hannah would be happy, my family was whole, and that was all that mattered to me.

"What about Nial? What do I tell the Prime?" I turned to the monster on the other examination table and clenched my jaw. Nial was nearly covered with metallic grafts and devices, some protruding from his skull from brain probes and implants. I'd seen this before, and worse. I'd rescued warriors from Hive centers in worse condition, but those warriors were always shipped to a medical station for treatment and I rarely saw them again.

But just because I didn't see them, didn't mean I wasn't aware of Nial's prognosis. Most men couldn't recover from the level of genetic manipulation Nial had suffered. He was more machine than man now. Hive.

Something of what I was thinking must have shown on my face because when I looked up, the doctor was watching me.

"He's not as bad as some I've seen. I'll get to work on him right away. Don't tell the Prime anything yet."

"When will you know?" Man or machine? Could the prince survive without the added technology? Had they wiped out too many of his natural systems?

"When I pull the probes from his brain stem."

A jolt of cold panic struck through my collar and Dare groaned from his exam table. "Hannah." He tried to sit up, brought back to consciousness by our mate's fear.

I didn't bother with explanations, simply ran from the room, with Dare staggering behind me.

The doctor yelled at Dare to stop, but I knew my second. Our mate was in trouble. Unless he was dead, he would fight beside me to save her.

Hannah

I froze for a moment, then pulled my hand back to my lap and turned to look up at Harbart. I knew the moment Zane felt my fear, and his rage gave me courage. He was coming. I just had to stall the crazy for a couple of minutes. "You're insane, Harbart. What do you want from me?"

"You need to die. Nial will die. I'll make sure of that. And then the commander will take my daughter as his bride, as he should have when I offered her to him."

I shook my head, confused. "But Prince Nial will be Prime. Why would you want a commander, when you can have the ruler of the whole planet?"

Harbart scoffed at me as if I were an ignorant child. "Commander Deston controls the entire interstellar fleet, little human. Warriors from *hundreds* of worlds bow to his command." He stepped forward and grabbed me by my hair, pulling me half off the floor as tears stung my eyes and my scalp burned. "As they will obey yours, *Lady Deston*, once the claiming ceremony is complete."

I reached for his hand, trying to hold on and take some

of my body weight off my hair. "I don't understand. Just let me go."

"Of course you don't, stupid human girl." He dragged me toward the door and I tried to keep my feet under me but failed. "Our warriors rule in war, but their mates rule in peace."

What the hell did that mean? My vision was blurred with tears as Harbart stepped to the door. He was forced to stop to wait for it to open and I knew this was my only chance. I scrambled until I had my feet under me, then used one hard kick to crumble Harbart's knee from behind. He fell back, letting go of my hair to land partially on top of me. The weapon went flying from his hand and I shoved at his huge body trying to get him off me so I could reach it first.

"You bitch. I'll strangle you with my bare hands."

His huge hands wrapped around my leg and dragged me toward him. I kicked at his face, my fingernails trying to claw their way through the floor to gain traction.

The door opened and my mates burst into the room. Zane's roar blasted through my body and I crumbled in relief as my mate lifted Harbart from the floor and threw him across the room. The old man hit the wall with a sickening crunch and I knew his skull hadn't survived the impact, but Zane wasn't finished with him.

I buried my face in my arm until a pair of strong, familiar hands wrapped around me. "Come, love. Let's get you to medical while Zane takes care of this."

Dare lifted me in his arms and I let him carry me out of the room, Harbart's screams drifting to us down the corridor.

CHAPTER FOURTEEN

Hannah

With a smile on my face, I watched my mates enter the medical station and question poor Doctor Mordin as if my health were vital to the survival of entire planets, not just to the claiming ceremony that was scheduled to begin in the next few minutes.

I was sitting in the medical station wearing nothing but a white robe and the collar around my neck. It was black, but not long from now, I'd have both of my mates filling me, claiming me, and it would turn a dark, beautiful red.

In the bed next to mine, Prince Nial sat with his back propped up by half a dozen pillows. I glanced at him from the corner of my eye, pleased to see him grin as Zane asked the same question for the third time.

I laughed, happy and eager to get to the ceremony. "Zane, I'm fine. I don't want to delay the ceremony."

Both of my mates turned to me and my breath caught in my throat. God, they were beautiful, both of them. They wore dark red robes that matched their collars, and nothing else. Their size alone should have scared me, but a shiver of desire made my pussy clench. My mates. *Mine*. Dare, so tender and gentle when I needed it, so sensual and patient in bed, made me laugh and calmed me when I needed to feel cherished. Zane, his power and mastery of me made me feel safe and protected and *needed*. Dare loved me, I could feel the warmth of his emotions like hot rays of the sun shining on my soul. But Zane's love was more like an inferno of lust and need, of power and surrender. Zane was my anchor, my matched mate, my master. Without Zane, I would truly be lost.

He came to me and lifted his hand to my chin, turning my face to make sure all the bruising was gone. "Are you in pain, mate? I will not do this if you are not healed."

I slapped his hand away, irritated to be having this conversation again. "I'm fine. Those ReGen things healed me most of the way. I'm a little bruised, but I don't care, Zane. I want you to be mine forever. I want you both to be mine. I don't want to wait."

Dare walked to stand beside Zane, his arms crossed over his massive chest. "Hannah, we will decide when you are ready. The doctor—"

"No! I decide. Not him. Me. You." I hopped down off the table and poked Zane in the chest with my finger. "If you don't want me, fine. I'll go home. But—"

Zane shut me up with a kiss. Dare chuckled. The doctor sighed with relief and Prince Nial cleared his throat.

"Zane, cousin, I have one request before you go."

Zane ended the kiss and pulled me into his side, his arm around my waist and I settled there, content as a kitten. God, I loved him. So much. So damn much.

"What do you need, Nial?"

The prince looked embarrassed, as much as he could with the odd metallic sheen that remained on the left side of his face. His left eye was a strange silver, and he had metallic implants in his left arm and leg. He looked like a half-finished cyborg, like something out of a *Star Trek* movie I'd seen once where a weird alien race of machines took people and took over their bodies with gadgets and computer programming. It was creepy and weird, but the look in the prince's good eye made me sad. He looked lost.

"I require transport to Earth, and a ship in that sector once I arrive. I can't go back to Prillon like this. And the doctor informed me yesterday that my matched mate was selected, from Earth, just like you, Hannah. But she was denied transport due to my... condition."

I gasped. "But Harbart's daughter—"

"Was never going to happen, not after I saw you with the commander." Prince Nial looked at Zane with a sad smile. "I didn't understand what you meant about not wanting a political match, cousin, until I saw you with her. Now I understand. I want my mate. She's mine."

Zane's arm tensed around me. "You want to go after her? She may not come willingly."

The prince looked Zane in the eye. "I will have her, Zane. With or without your help. She's my mate."

"Very well. Doctor?" Zane shouted for Doctor Mordin over his shoulder, but the huge man was standing right behind Dare.

"I've got it all recorded, commander. I'll take care of it."

Zane held out his hand, the one not around me, and Nial took it.

"Good luck. I hope you find her."

"I will. Thank you."

Zane let him go and looked down at me. I was so eager for my men I could barely stand still.

"Let's go, Hannah. It's time for you to claim your mates."

Zane led me from the room and I walked between him and Dare in the long corridor until we reached the claiming room. I looked around in wonder, anticipation making my pussy wet before I'd cleared the door.

"Stand in the center of the room and face us." Zane issued the order and I hurried to comply. When I reached the center I stopped and took a quick look around. The room was bare except for one small cushion in the center, but it wasn't something I'd ever seen on a couch back home.

No, this cushion was the size of a bed and hip high, just the right height for Dare to take me from behind while I rode Zane's cock.

I shuddered as heat flooded my system and Zane cleared his throat, drawing my gaze from the bed thing back to him. Dare stood beside him, shoulder to shoulder, and I admired the view as both of my mates dropped their robes to the floor and stood before me naked. Behind them a curved black glass hid other men, my mate's chosen warriors, from my view. They were here to witness the claiming and pledge their lives to mine.

I didn't know who was back there and I didn't care. I wanted to claim my men forever. I wanted them to fuck me, stretch me, and make me beg—

Zane spoke. "You will only be asked two questions, Hannah. The first," he nodded to Dare, who held up a length of black cloth.

"Do you wish your eyes to be covered, or do you wish to see?"

Wow! So, Anne had faced this same choice?

I remembered the sensation of waiting to know what her mates would do, the anticipation, the not knowing— "Blindfolded."

"Drop your robe." I did and Zane's knowing look made my insides melt like butter on a hot plate as Dare approached, his cock rock hard and ready to take me. Dare stepped behind me and I held Zane's gaze until the last possible moment as Dare covered my eyes and secured the soft cloth behind my head. He took my hand and led me to the cushion where I found Zane's strong hands waiting to cup my breasts. I stopped with a moan and Dare moved in behind me, plastering his heated flesh to my back as Zane squeezed and pinched my nipples.

"Hold her." Zane's rough command made me go limp as wet heat flooded my pussy.

"My pleasure." Dare's voice whispered against my ear as his arms trapped mine to my sides. He rubbed his huge cock against my ass over and over, a teaser of what was to come. I whimpered and pushed back into him. "Soon, love. Soon I will be fucking you until you scream for us."

I heard Zane moving and bit my lip to keep myself from crying out to him to hurry up. The warriors hidden behind the dark screens began the chant I remembered from the simulation at the bride processing center and my entire body was electric with memories. I was about to cry with frustration when Dare lifted me completely off my feet and sat me down on top of Zane. My mate was lying on his back and I was now straddling his thighs, his huge cock pressed to my clit in the front and I rolled my hips, trying to rub along his hard length. Strong hands clamped onto my thighs, careful of the bruise I still carried from Harbart's evil, and I knew then, in that moment, that my mates would never hurt me, never leave me, never cheat on me or take me for granted.

Zane's deep voice, his words rumbled up through me from his chest. "Do you accept my claim, mate? Do you give yourself to me and my second freely, or do you wish to choose another primary mate?"

"I accept your claim, warriors." The moment I said the words, Dare stepped close again and I realized he was behind me, ready to take me from behind as I rode Zane, taking his huge cock deep.

"Then we claim you in the rite of naming. You are mine and I shall kill any other warrior who dares to touch you."

"I love you, Hannah. Always." Dare pressed his lips to the side of my face as the voices I'd heard chanting earlier answered him in a ritual sounding chorus of male voices.

"May the gods witness and protect you."

I had less than a second to swoon and go soft for Dare's declaration before Zane pulled me forward for a kiss. Dare took advantage of the situation and spread my cheeks to insert the lube in my ass as Zane fucked my mouth with his tongue. He placed my hands behind my back and held them there with one of his own; the other was free to pull on my ass, lifting it into the air for Dare to play.

Zane stole my air as Dare slid three fingers inside me and another below, finger fucking me and rubbing my clit at the same time. He rubbed his pre-cum on my ass cheek and the magical substance sank into my skin and heated my blood until it felt like lava flowing in my veins.

I was on the edge of an orgasm, riding Dare's fingers with wild abandon until Zane wrapped his hand around the back of my neck and gently pulled. "Not until you have permission, mate."

His command drove me higher and I whimpered. I knew the NPU was recording this for the bride program. I knew that there were at least a half dozen men watching and I didn't care. I wanted my mates to fuck me, fill me, make me theirs forever.

Dare's hands left me and Zane held me perfectly still, an empty, aching mess.

I considered arguing with my men, as Anne had done, telling them to hurry, ordering them about so I could feel the burn of their hard strikes on my bare ass, but I knew that was not what Zane wanted. He didn't want me to push him; he wanted me to give him everything.

His voice was soft, almost a whisper below me. "Tell me what you want, Hannah."

"You." That single word was a soul-deep confession, a complete surrender. "I want you. I want Dare."

He brought me back down until my lips were touching his, but not kissing. Contact. Nothing more. "Why?"

Why? "Because I love you, Zane. I love you. I love you both."

He crushed my lips to his and lifted my hips. Dare reached between us and placed Zane's cock at the opening of my pussy and Zane, mouth still locked to mine, lowered me onto his shaft with a shudder that racked his entire body.

Behind me, Dare stroked my ass with tender hands. "Are you ready for me, love?"

"Yes." God, yes. I was ready.

Dare pushed into me slowly, stretching me until I thought I would scream. As I panted, Zane kissed my cheeks and chin, my lips and nose and reached down to pull on my ass cheeks, spreading me wide for my second lover to fill me up.

I groaned at the double penetration, the tight feel of both men filling me.

When they were both fully seated, I reached up and gripped Zane's hair in tight fists, eager for them to move, for Zane to let me come. I needed him to give me permission. I needed my master to set me free.

Zane's hands ran up and down my back, petting me, soothing the pain, loving me. I stopped trying to guess what they would do next and simply laid my cheek down over Zane's heart, content to let him take me wherever he wanted me to go.

They alternated their thrusts, one filling me deep as the other retreated, lighting up nerves in my pussy and ass where I bit my lip to hold back. My orgasm didn't belong to me. It belonged to my men.

"I love you, Hannah Johnson from Earth." Zane's words brought tears to my eyes and I turned to press a kiss over his heart. When I did, his hips jerked below me and I cried out at the exquisite pleasure-pain of his thrust. With Dare's huge cock in my ass, and Zane's huge cock in my pussy, I was split open, spread wide and claimed.

He thrust again and Dare pulled out of my ass just barely before pushing back in. I whimpered, waiting for my master, waiting to please him.

"Come for me, Hannah. Make me yours forever."

I came on his command, lost in the sensations pulsing through my body and through the collars that connected us as one. I felt the heat of it, knew even through my blindfold that my collar had changed colors.

They fucked me until I couldn't breathe, until my body had nothing left, until I'd come so many times, so hard that I couldn't move.

And I loved every minute of it.

THE END

BONUS: CHAPTER ONE OF *CLAIMED BY HER MATES*

Leah Adams, Interstellar Bride Processing Center, Earth

I tried to fight the feelings. I truly did, but the cock filling me up just felt too good. I even tried to fight *him*, but all it got me was a set of leather cuffs around my wrists. I was on my hands and knees, my body pressed against a strange, padded table. My cuffs were linked to the rings set low so I could not move. I tugged once, twice, but there was no give. My ass tilted high in the air, my mate's cock deep inside me. It was like I was tied over an odd wooden horse while someone *rode* me. I was completely at his mercy and could do nothing but succumb to the power of his body as he took mine.

His cock might have been a part of him, flesh and blood—albeit very hard and very large—but he wielded it like a weapon designed to make me submit. Once he filled me with his seed, once his essence coated my inner walls, filled my womb, there would be no turning back. I would crave his touch and his taste. I would *need* him to fill me, to take me, to forever claim my body. Now, with him expertly stretching me wide, with my bare bottom burning from the sting of his hand and my pussy on fire from the touch of his expert tongue, I didn't want to resist him any longer.

I used to be afraid. Now, I simply hungered. Ached.

He wasn't cruel; the opposite in fact. As my mate's cock moved inside me, filling me completely from behind before retreating, again and again, my fear left me. I was his now. He would own me, body and soul, but he was strong, a warrior. He would protect me. And fuck me. He would keep me in line with his firm hand, but also bring me pleasure, and safety, and a home. All these thoughts flooded my mind as this powerful male made me his forever, his cock invading my body over and over as I opened for him.

His large hands skimmed my back before he bent over, covering me with the heat of a warrior's strength, resting his fingers beside mine where I was cuffed to the table. The longer he took me, the tighter his grip became on the handles, the whiter the knuckles.

His slick chest lay over my back, pinning me against the bench, adding to the sensation of being trapped. I couldn't even avoid his harsh breathing, the sounds of pleasure that escaped his lips, for they were right by my ear.

"Feel that?" he growled, shifting his hips and hitting my womb with the hard tip of his cock. He was adept at stroking over secret, sensitive places deep inside that made my body quake, my mind blank, my submission complete. There was no one else who could make me feel this way. No one else had ever pushed my body to the brink of the most delicious pleasure.

As I was positioned over the bench, my breasts hung down and ached to be touched. My clit was swollen and if he even brushed over it with just the tip of his finger, I would come. But he would deny me for now. He would deny me until I broke, until I begged.

I couldn't help the breathy "Yes" that escaped my lips. I could hear the wet sounds of fucking—the clearest sign of my arousal—fill the room.

"You feared my cock, but it only brings pleasure. I told you I'd fit, that we'd be perfect." He spoke as he fucked me. How did he know my body so well when this was our first time? I'd never come from a cock before, only rubbing my clit in bed, alone. But now that personal task would be denied me. My mate insisted that I never come without permission again. If I broke this rule, I would be spanked long and hard. Now that I belonged to him, I would come by his will, by his tongue, his hand, his huge cock… or not at all.

"Your pleasure is mine."

"Yes," I replied.

"I feel you squeezing me."

"Yes," I cried, clenching down on him once again. It was all I could say for I had no control anymore. I was completely at his mercy and all I wanted to do was exactly what he demanded.

"You will not come until I give you permission." He lifted his hands from the table to stroke my breasts, the softest caress first, then a hard tug and pinching that made me whimper as he pounded into me hard and fast and deep. It was a pain/pleasure he elicited and I loved it. "You are mine. Your pussy is mine."

"Yes," I repeated, again and again.

He didn't stop riding me, fucking me, filling me, taking me. Claiming me. Higher and higher I climbed until I tossed my head back and forth and I gripped the handles with desperation so great I feared my heart would explode in my chest. I couldn't breathe. Couldn't think. Couldn't resist. I was there, right… there. My mate's hand skimmed my down my hip, roaming the softly rounded flesh of my body until he reached my clit. He traced the edges with his finger and the sound that left my throat was the soft scream of a creature in agony, frantic and lost. Nothing existed for me but his body, his voice, his breath, his touch.

"Come now," he commanded, his cock like a piston, his

fingers on my clit hard and unforgiving.

My orgasm exploded deep within me, for I had no other choice. I couldn't resist it. I had no control. I was no longer myself, I was his. I screamed my release, my body clenching and releasing around his cock, pulling him in deeper, holding him all the way inside me. It was as if my body craved his life essence, was desperate for it.

My release triggered his and I felt him swell and grow even bigger before he growled in my ear, hot pulses of his seed filling me. My body greedily milked his cock of the life essence, taking it deep inside.

Just as he'd promised, something in his seed triggered a physical reaction in me, forcing me to come a second time.

"Yes, love. Yes, take every drop. Your body is changing. It knows me. It must have me. You will beg for my cock; you will crave my seed. You will need it, love it, just as I need and love you."

"Yes!" I cried again, knowing his words were true. It was a hot wash of pleasure that seeped through my body, directly from my pussy, then outward. He was right; now that I felt the power of him, of what he could give me, I was a slave to it. I was a slave to his cock.

"Miss Adams?"

"Yes," I said once again, my dream merging with the present.

"Miss Adams, your testing is over."

I shook my head. No. I was bound to a fucking bench and being fucked and filled with seed. I wanted to stay there. I wanted... more.

"Miss Adams!"

The voice was stern now, and loud. I forced my eyes open.

"Oh, God," I gasped, trying to catch my breath as my pussy clenched and pulsed with aftershocks of my orgasms. I wasn't tied down to a fucking bench. No solid male body pressed into my back. I was in the Interstellar Bride Program's processing center in a medical examination

155

gown. My wrists were trapped in medical restraints secured to the edges of an uncomfortable reclining chair, similar to a dentist's, for the last stage of preparations for going off-planet. I hadn't realized, when they'd hooked up the wires and sensors, that I would end up in a sex dream. I felt the lingering effects of it. My pussy was wet, the back of my scratchy medical gown damp. My nipples were hard and my hands were clenched into fists. I felt wrung out and used. I felt complete.

"As I said, your testing is over." Warden Egara stood before me. A stern young woman with dark brown hair and a hawk-like attention to every detail of the matching process, she glanced down at her tablet as her finger ran over it. "Your match has been made."

I licked my dry lips as I tried to slow my frantic heart. Goosebumps broke out on my sweaty skin. "The dream... was it real?"

"It wasn't a dream," she replied, her tone matter-of-fact. "We use recorded sensory data from prior brides to assist in the matching process."

"What?" Recorded data?

"A neuro-processing unit, or NPU, will be inserted in your skull before you leave Earth. It assists in language and helps you adapt to your new world." She grinned then, and the sight was as frightening as it was wicked. "The NPU is programmed to record your mating and send the data back to the system."

"You are going to record me with my new mate?"

"Yes. That is required by the matching protocol. All claiming ceremonies are reviewed to ensure that our brides are safely and properly placed." She dropped the tablet to her side and I noticed the stiff collar and starched skirt of her uniform. There was not a wrinkle to be seen, not a single hair out of place in her tight chignon. She looked almost like a robot. But the fire in her eyes betrayed her fervor and dedication to her duty. Her devotion to the program was clearly evident in her next words. "We do all we can to make sure our warriors receive worthy brides. They serve us all, protecting the Earth and all member planets from certain destruction. The system uses your body's reactions to probe your inner conscience, your darkest fantasies, your innermost needs. What didn't interest you was quickly discarded by the matching program. The sensory input was filtered until we found a warrior from a planet with a perfect match."

That had been my match? Surely not. "I can't be matched to a man who ties me up. That's not what I wanted when I volunteered."

Her dark eyebrow winged up at that. "Apparently, Miss Adams, that is exactly what you desire. The testing reveals the truth, even if your mind denies it."

I thought of her words as she moved around the table and took a seat opposite me. Her crisp uniform for the Interstellar Bride Program matched her cool demeanor. "You are an unusual case, Miss Adams. While we do have a few volunteers, we have never had one with your reasons before."

I glanced at the closed door for a moment, worried that perhaps she'd called my fiancé and had sent for him. Sheer panic had me tugging at the restraints.

"Do not worry," she said, her one hand raised to stop me. "You are safe here. While you've stated that the bruises on your body are from a fall, I felt it necessary to ensure that no one be allowed to see you before I send you off-planet."

Obviously Warden Egara didn't believe my ridiculous story, and I was reassured by her vehemence in protecting me. I'd never skied in my life. I didn't even live anywhere near a mountain, but a reasonable excuse was required for the bruises on my body and it was the first thing that came to mind.

While I'd assumed the bruises would be uncovered, I'd had no idea that I would be stripped bare for medical tests, then placed in a hospital gown and put through a screening of completely inappropriate images and motion clips. I must have fallen asleep, for I could not have imagined any of it on my own.

"Thank you," I replied.

I wasn't used to people being kind. She remained quiet as if waiting for me to tell her the truth. Did I want to share what I knew now about my fiancé? He'd been so kind, sweeping me off my feet, until I learned the truth. I'd overheard him telling one of his men to kill someone who had made one of his real estate deals fall through. I'd thought the men he kept around were employees, bodyguards, but they were enforcers, men he used to intimidate and kill. Once I'd agreed to marry him, he'd assigned two of his men as my personal *bodyguards*. Even then I'd believed the reason was simply that he was rich and I needed extra protection. I'd thought him considerate and caring, watching out for me. Ha! I'd been so *stupid*. Even more stupid when I told him I was having second thoughts about our wedding. He'd gone ballistic, grabbed me and told me he was never letting me go. Never.

When I threatened to leave, he quietly and fervently explained that he owned me. I was his property as soon as I'd placed his engagement ring on my finger. He'd kill anyone I kissed, torture any man who touched me, and then punish me for the trouble.

I knew then I had to get away, but I'd have to find a way to escape. I'd gone to the mall in my car as if it were a normal day. The men who watched me always parked their car beside mine, followed me through the mall, but allowed me to roam inside the stores alone. Just in case, I veered directly for the lingerie department where I knew they always backed off, then weaved through several other stores, dropping my cell phone between two racks of clothes. I hurried to the bus stop and took the bus across town. From there I'd hired a taxi to the Interstellar Bride Program's processing center.

I had no family, no friends left. When we'd begun dating he'd systematically removed everyone from my life I had cared about before I met him. One by one, he'd offered reasons for why they were no longer appropriate, no longer acceptable contacts. I was totally and completely alone in the world now, at his mercy. He'd even convinced me to give up my job, so I had no money of my own.

God help me, but even an alien was better than a psychotic, possessive man whose idea of punishment involved boxing practice, with me as the punching bag. I'd suffered it once. Never again. I might have been foolish, naïve, and even a little love-struck, but no longer.

I'd looked over my shoulder the entire trip to the processing center, afraid they'd track me down and stop me before I could enter the building. Once within the walls I felt safer, but I wouldn't feel completely out of their reach until I was off-planet. Only then would I breathe easy, confident that my fiancé could never find me.

I'd heard about the Interstellar Bride Program for over a year, knowing that most women who participated were prisoners seeking an alternative to a harsh prison sentence. Some, I'd learned, were volunteers, but none could return. Once matched to an alien warrior and sent off-planet to their mate, they were no longer citizens of Earth and could not return. At first, it had sounded scary and ridiculous. Who would *volunteer* to leave Earth? How bad could their lives be to do such a thing? Now I knew. A woman's life could turn very, *very* bad.

I needed to be as far away from my fiancé as possible and I worried that there would be no place on Earth that would be far enough. He would find me, then…

I'd thought he would be my family. *Family.* He'd chosen me to be his wife because I had none. I had no ties, no one to protect me, to keep me from marrying the asshole. He would never be my family. No one on Earth held any love for me. As a volunteer of the bride program, I was glad to know I couldn't return. I didn't want to be on Earth any longer. I didn't want to have the fear of him hunting me lingering for the remainder of my life. And so I would go off-planet, to the only place he could never find me, never reach me again.

And so here I sat, in a scratchy gown, under the scrutiny of Warden Egara.

"Do you have questions?"

I licked my lips again. "This match... how do I know he will be... nice?" While I'd been put through so many tests for the matching, my only requirement was that he was nice. I didn't want to be mated to a man who beat me. If I wanted that, I could just stay here on Earth and marry the asshole.

"Nice? Miss Adams, I believe I understand the depth of your concern, but your mate has been put through the same tests. In fact, the warriors are required to submit to more advanced testing than our brides. You do not need to fear your match, for your subconscious minds are what determine a match. Your needs and desires complement one another. However, you must remember, a different planet has different customs. A different culture. You will need to adjust to this, to reject your Earthly judgments and antiquated notions. You will need to set aside your fear of men. Leave them here on Earth."

The words were wise, but the deed not so easily done. I would be cautious for a long time, I was sure. "Where am I going?"

"Viken."

I frowned. "I've never heard of the planet."

"Mmm," she replied, looking down at her table. "You are the first from Earth to be matched there. The dreams you saw were a female from another planet and her matched Viken. As you saw, he was an attentive, yet thorough lover."

I blushed at the memory.

"Based on this testing, I think you will be very pleased with your mate."

"And if I'm not?" What if she was wrong and he was mean? He might be able to wield his cock like porn star, but what if he wanted me to be nothing more than a slave to him? What if he beat me like my fiancé did?

"You have thirty days to change your mind," she answered. "Keep in mind you have been matched not only to a man, but to the planet. If you do not find your match acceptable after thirty days, you may request another warrior, but you will remain on Viken."

That seemed reasonable. I sighed, relaxing at the notion that I could make my own choice in the end—and not be sent back to Earth.

"You are satisfied?" she asked. "Do you have more questions? Is there any reason to delay your transport?"

She looked to me as if offering me one last opportunity. An opportunity I would not take. "No. There is no reason to delay."

She nodded her head. "Very good. For the record, Miss Adams, are you married?"

"No." If I hadn't gotten away, I would have been. In two weeks.

"Do you have any children?"

"No."

"Good." She swiped her screen again. "You have been formally matched to the planet Viken. Do you accept the match?"

"Yes," I replied. As long as the man wasn't mean, I would go anywhere to escape.

"Because of your affirmative response, you have been officially matched and are now stripped of your citizenship of Earth. You are now, and will forever be, a bride of Viken." She glanced down at her screen, swiped her finger over it. "Per Viken custom, some modifications to your body are required before your transport."

Warden Egara stood and came around beside me.

"Modifications?" What did that mean? What was she going to do?

She pushed a button on the wall above my head, which made it slide open. Glancing over my shoulder, I couldn't see more than soft blue lighting. What I did notice was the large arm that extended out from the wall with a needle attached. "What's that?"

"No need to be afraid. We are simply implanting your NPU, required for all brides. Hold still. It only takes a few seconds."

The robotic arm came toward me and poked into my neck. I winced at the surprise of it, but it didn't truly hurt. In fact, nothing hurt. As the chair moved backward into the room with the blue light, I was relaxed and calm, sleepy.

"You have nothing to fear any longer, Miss Adams." As the chair lowered into a warm bath, she added. "Your processing will begin in three… two… one."

Printed in Great Britain
by Amazon